**Also by Dana Reinhardt**

*A Brief Chapter in My Impossible Life*

*Harmless*

# HOW TO BUILD A HOUSE

## a novel by

## Dana Reinhardt

WENDY
LAMB
BOOKS

All rights reserved. Published by Wendy Lamb Books, an imprint of Random House Children's Books, a division of Random House, Inc., New York. Originally published in hardcover in the United States by Wendy Lamb Books in 2008.

Wendy Lamb Books and the colophon are trademarks of Random House, Inc.

Visit us on the Web! www.randomhouse.com/teens

Educators and librarians, for a variety of teaching tools, visit us at www.randomhouse.com/teachers

The Library of Congress has cataloged the hardcover edition of this work as follows:
Reinhardt, Dana.
  How to build a house / Dana Reinhardt.
    p. cm.
Summary: Seventeen-year-old Harper Evans hopes to escape the effects of her father's divorce on her family and friendships by volunteering her summer to build a house in a small Tennessee town devastated by a tornado.
  ISBN 978-0-375-84453-9 (hc) — ISBN 978-0-375-94454-3 (glb)
— ISBN 978-0-375-89388-9 (e-book)
  [1. Building—Fiction. 2. Interpersonal relations—Fiction. 3. Divorce—Fiction.
4. Stepfamilies—Fiction. 5. Voluntarism—Fiction. 6. Tennessee—Fiction.] I. Title.
PZ7.R2753How 2008
[Fic]—dc22
2007033403

ISBN: 978-0-375-84454-6 (tr. pbk.)

Printed in the United States of America

10 9 8 7 6 5 4 3

First Trade Paperback Edition

*This book is for my parents.*

# HOW TO BUILD A HOUSE

# STEP ONE:
# SELECT THE PERFECT SITE

The world is drowning.

Sinking.

It's being swallowed up. Glaciers are melting. Oceans are rising.

It's an indisputable fact: We're ruining the planet.

I'm finding it hard to keep this in mind gazing out my window. From where I'm sitting things look, well, dry. The earth looks *thirsty*. All I can see is dusty brown. Miles and miles of it stretching on forever.

Here comes a flight attendant now with her big block of a metal cart to ask me if I'd like something to drink.

If *I'm* thirsty.

I order a diet root beer. She smiles. Diet root beer is not a beverage she keeps in the recesses of her metal cart.

Okay. Make it a Diet Sprite.

Out of luck again.

I take water. No ice.

I swore off regular soda about a month ago and took up the diet variety. This has nothing to do with my body image, which I'll confess, like most of us, isn't exactly stellar. But this is about something bigger than just my thighs. It's about the national obesity epidemic. It's about taking a stand against the sugar water that's turning our children into Oompa-Loompas.

So I stopped.

I know diet soda isn't great for you either, but you have to start somewhere. And anyway, right now I'm drinking water. No ice.

We're about an hour away.

I've flown over this part of the country before. Many times. When you live in California and you have relatives in New York, everything in between feels like a big inconvenience. It's what keeps *you* from *them*, or *here* from *there*, and you want it out of your way as quickly as possible because your headphones aren't working, and anyway you've already seen the movie three times.

But today I'm watching that big inconvenience and how it's changed from a flat, endless grid of look-alike houses to snowcapped mountains to red valleys to dusty brown, thirsty earth. Today I'm waiting to be dropped down in the middle of it.

Tennessee.

To be more precise, I'm going to Bailey, Tennessee, which almost nobody has ever heard of.

If you watch TV or read the newspaper or if you have a pulse, then you know about what happened in New Orleans. You know about the hurricane with the name of a princess that left the city underwater.

But that wasn't the world's last catastrophe.

Catastrophes come, and they come. They come in all shapes and sizes, one after the other, lined up like planes in the sky, waiting for their turn to land. The tornado in Bailey came this past April, and nobody paid attention except for one small organization with a teen volunteer program where I am spending my summer vacation.

Sure, the tornado in Bailey wreaked havoc on the lives of an insignificant number of people when you compare it to Hurricane Katrina, but when it's your life . . . I doubt it feels insignificant to you.

Tornadoes. They're just another indication that the planet is going to hell in a handbasket. A handbasket that's been meticulously crafted and woven by us, the backward-looking members of the human race. If it weren't for how we're ruining things with our trash and our gas emissions and the way we're turning the planet into an Easy-Bake Oven, there might not have even been a category F4 tornado in Bailey, Tennessee.

Then again, maybe it would have come anyway.

Tornadoes can happen out of nowhere. Without warning.

# HOME

It's one of those sad stories. I hesitate to even talk about it, because when I do, people start to feel sorry for me, and that isn't necessary.

My mother died when I was two.

Okay. Now I've said it. Now I can get that out of the way.

The important thing is that my dad didn't die. He lived. He still lives. In fact, right now he's probably back at his office, after fighting through traffic from the airport, listening to one of his patients drone on and on, staring out the window. And then he'll see a plane flying overhead with a white, gauzy streak trailing behind it, and he'll wonder why it seemed like a good idea to let me go all the way to Tennessee for the summer.

This isn't the first time I've run away.

Once, when we were about eight, Tess and I stuffed a backpack with a towel, some socks and a box of Lucky Charms. We figured what's the point in running away unless someone knows about it?

So we told Dad.

He said fine. Just remember, you aren't allowed to cross the street.

We stopped at the corner and ate a few handfuls of stale Lucky Charms before turning. We turned the next corner, and the next, until we arrived back where we'd started: at our own front door.

It isn't like that now. I'm running away, and I'm not only crossing the street, I'm crossing this dried-out country and I won't be back for twelve weeks and Dad is going to miss me because he'll be all alone.

Tess is gone.

So is Rose.

So, of course, is Jane.

He has Cole, sure, but Cole is only six, and what kind of company is a six-year-old who talks to insects? Especially when Dad sees him only some weekends and every other Wednesday night?

I guess I should start at the beginning.

There are so many beginnings to choose from. There's me and my birth almost eighteen years ago with my umbilical cord wrapped around my neck, a detail Dad likes to remind me about when I do something particularly boneheaded. There's Mom's death, which although it's an ending, the Big Ending, is also the beginning of my life without a mom. Then there's when Dad met Jane and the beginning of the only family I've ever known.

Yes. I'll start there.

◦ ◦ ◦

I would hide behind his legs.

I know the backs of Dad's knees, the way they feel against the top of my head, almost as well as I know the sound of his voice. I spent years of my life there, my arms locked around his calves, while he would say with mock befuddlement, "Has anyone seen Harper?"

Then I met Jane and I came out of hiding.

We went for a picnic at the beach. It was a perfectly gloomy day.

June Gloom.

It's an expression you hear often growing up in Southern California. I always imagined June Gloom as a character, an irresistibly spunky and wisecracking kid with pale skin and flyaway hair.

I was five. So was Tess. Rose was seven.

Dad said he wanted me to meet his friend Jane. She was a very "special" friend, he told me. Not the kind of special you might be if the umbilical cord gets pulled a little too tight around your neck at birth, but the kind of special that meant he ironed my sunflower dress for me that morning.

Her blanket was striped the colors of a rainbow that had no business at the beach on such a gloomy day.

There was fried chicken, macaroni and cheese, corn on the cob and chocolate pudding. Basically a greatest hits of my favorite foods when I was five, and I guess this should have been my first indication that something important was going on with Dad and Jane.

Tess and Rose were down at the water's edge, playing a game of tag with the chilly gray surf. The wind blew their long hair around their faces and tangled it together so they looked like a two-bodied creature, connected by this mass of moving hair, black as the bottom of the ocean.

"You must be Cinderella," Jane said, and did a little bow. She wore chunky silver rings on her fingers and big dangling earrings. "It's such a pleasure to meet you, Your Highness."

"Nooooo." I giggled from my spot behind Dad's knees.

"Sleeping Beauty?"

"Nope."

"Ah, you must be Snow White."

"No. I'm Harper." I stepped to the side and scoped out the picnic spread.

"Good thing, because that's what this crown says." And she took from her bag a paper crown decorated with plastic jewels, my name spelled out in glitter.

Jane turned toward the water and whistled. One long loud whistle followed by three short ones. It would become the whistle she'd use to call me too if I was far away. One long. Three short.

Tess and Rose came running, red-cheeked and sandy.

There were crowns for them too, and later there were pink pedicures and juice drunk from big silver goblets.

When I spilled my juice on my sunflower dress, Jane reached into her bag and pulled out a dry one. Purple eyelet.

Dad never thought to bring a change of clothes.

"That's my dress," Tess said. "It's my favorite one." She brought her eyebrows together and turned to me with what looked like a glare. Then she tucked her hair behind her

ears. She studied my face. She smiled. "But you can borrow it."

After Jane zipped it up in the back, Tess grabbed my hand.
"C'mon. The water's freezing. Let's go!"

We ran down to the surf after Rose, where the wind did
little to move my new pageboy haircut with the too-short
bangs.

There would be many more dinners in our future orga-
nized around a theme. Chinese New Year with pajamas from
Chinatown and parasols and dumplings. Cinco de Mayo with
sombreros and paper flowers and enchiladas. But our first
themed dinner, dubbed the Royal Feast, took place on a
June Gloom afternoon, the gray sky punctuated by a bright
rainbow-striped blanket and pink toenails.

## HERE

We're landing now. Dusty brown has morphed into lush
green.

No matter how many times I fly or wherever I go in all my
life, I don't think the experience of watching the earth draw
closer will ever lose any of its beauty.

A note about how I got here, and I don't mean the flight.
What I mean is the *why* of how I got here.

I want to help. There are people whose homes have been
destroyed. Their lives uprooted. Everything gone. And I want
to help.

That's the easy answer.

That's the answer that convinces your dad to write that check to Homes from the Heart Summer Program for Teens.

Then there's the other answer.

The one about needing to run away.

There are too many things to run away from. There's what's happened to Dad and Jane and how what happened to them happened to everybody in our family. There's Gabriel and how everything between us seems to add up to nothing. There's Tess and who she is and isn't to me anymore. There's the way I feel when I wake up in the morning in my empty house. There are the days I walk down the halls at school and I can't even hear my own footsteps. There's the space that's opened up inside me, blooming slowly, like a large black flower.

But also, I do want to help. That answer is no less true just because it's the obvious one.

And anyway, I know a thing or two about people whose homes have been destroyed. Their lives uprooted. Everything gone.

◯ ◯ ◯

I'm looking for a sign.

One with my name on it, somewhere near baggage claim. I'm not speaking metaphorically.

I'm here. Finally.

I collect my suitcase and still, no sign.

Instinctively I reach into the side pocket of my backpack,

into the little compartment designed to hold my cell phone. It's empty. It's one of the rules for all the teen volunteers this summer: no cell phones.

And even if I did bring a cell phone to Tennessee, who would I call? I'm standing smack-dab in the middle of the big inconvenience.

I don't know a soul.

This realization has the surprise effect of calming my nerves.

*I don't know a soul.*

Then I see it.

H. EVANS

The man holding the sign is tall with red hair and a red beard. I've never met a lumberjack, and I'm not really sure if they're real or imaginary, but the first thing that comes to mind when I see this man holding a sign with my name on it is that he looks like a lumberjack to me.

He squints when he sees me walking toward him.

"I'm H. Evans."

"I figured. I'm Linus." He sticks out his hand and I shake it. "Welcome to Memphis International Airport."

"Uh, thanks."

"I'm your Homes group leader for the summer."

I know this already. I read the short paragraph about him that came with the paperwork. I read all the paperwork. I'm nothing if not thorough.

Linus Devereaux. The paragraph said he's built homes in Alaska, Mississippi, the Florida Gulf Coast, South Dakota,

Watts, Haiti, the Congo and the Ukraine. It didn't say anything else about him, but it did end with this quote from Gandhi that all the posers at school like to put on their senior yearbook pages: "You must be the change you wish to see in the world."

Then again, those posers go off to UCLA or USC or sometimes Yale, and they drink too much and throw up out their dorm windows, and this guy is off building houses in every corner of the globe, so I guess maybe he's actually earned the right to put Gandhi's quote beneath a picture of himself with an uncomfortable smile.

I wasn't in the brochure. No picture, no biographical information.

*Harper Evans lives in Los Angeles, California, with her father. And sometimes her little brother. And sometimes the family border collie. And nobody else.*

We walk through the terminal until we reach the baggage claim area for another airline and now Linus holds a sign that says F. GREGORY.

Linus the Lumberjack smiles at me. "I hope you're not in too much of a hurry."

"Not at all. I'm just happy for the lift. I'm a little out of my element here."

"Most of you will be, I'd guess. We've got lots of city kids coming. Kids from all over. There's plenty to learn, but we'll help you through. And we'll ply you with plenty of Advil."

Seeing my quizzical look, he adds, "The muscles tend to go into a wee bit of shock during the first days of work."

"Sounds like fun."

"It is."

Linus looks down at the signs in his hands. "We'll be on the road soon. Two more of you coming in. And I've just noticed that you kept it easy on me by arriving in alphabetical order."

"Yeah, we planned it that way. Me and F. Gregory. He called me to make sure I caught an early flight."

"It's a she."

"Oops."

"You had a fifty percent chance of getting that right."

"Actually, I had a fifty-point-seven percent chance."

"Those are good odds."

"I thought so too."

I sit down on my suitcase and grab my backpack and again I reach for the phone that isn't there. It's a reflex. An addiction.

Dad and I have a thing. Whenever I arrive wherever it is I'm going, I call to tell him I got there. It's a little neurotic, I know, but you can't really blame him when you consider what happened to Mom.

Linus reaches into the leather case attached to his belt, pulls out a cell phone and tosses it to me. I catch it one-handed. "Call your father," he says.

I check myself. Did I say something out loud? I could have sworn I was just *thinking* about how I needed to call Dad. Maybe I've become one of those annoying people who mutter. God, I hope this isn't true.

I take this as an opportunity to step outside.

Tennessee heat is brutal. I've been told it's not the heat, it's the humidity. A distinction I've never understood until right this very moment.

I'm wearing this heat like a heavy, damp blanket.

Dad picks up right away and sounds relieved when he hears my voice, but also different.

Small.

Like a miniature version of Dad.

"I'm here. In the airport. I haven't seen any more of Tennessee, but the airport's perfectly nice."

"I really miss you," he says.

I feel my lungs filling up with something I don't recognize. I can scarcely breathe.

"I have to go. Other people are arriving. In alphabetical order."

"Listen, I know we have a rule about me not going through your things and generally keeping my hands and eyes off of anything that belongs to you, so please, let me humbly seek your forgiveness for having slipped a little something into your backpack. The inside zippered pocket."

"You went through my stuff?"

"I opened the zipper with my eyes closed, but I couldn't help having to touch a few things."

"Dad. I'm joking."

"I know."

"I really do have to go."

"I know that too."

I snap the phone closed and stare at it while the blanket of heat wraps itself tighter around me.

## HOME

At the wedding I wore white.

The dress had no sleeves and a bow that tied in the back.

It was a small party, held in our backyard. Jane's friend Daniel, a rabbinical school dropout, performed the ceremony. He drew on the Jewish rituals important to Jane while also making it a comfortable experience for my atheist father.

Me? I didn't care about rituals or God or vows. I just loved my dress and couldn't wait to get my hands on that cake.

We danced outside. The grass was damp because Dad forgot to turn off the sprinklers that morning, so we all went barefoot. I remember the hem of my dress getting splattered with mud and stained from the grass and how I started to panic until Jane came over and took me by the hands, and the look on her face was so calm and content and happy that a rare moment of rationality took hold of my six-year-old self, and I decided nothing as silly as stains on white tulle could ruin the day.

It was perfect.

They'd moved into our house about two months before. I was thrilled to share a room with Tess. I'd always wanted bunk beds. The problem was, so had she, and like me, she had her heart set on the top bunk, so we settled for twin beds on opposite sides of the room, and this arrangement put a halt to my pattern of waking up in the middle of the night not knowing where I was.

They moved in one day, and the next it was as if they'd been there forever.

I know how that sounds. It sounds ridiculous. Like a lie. The hallways should have echoed with the shrill screams of bickering girls. Doors should have slammed. Harsh words spoken. Feelings bruised.

That would all come later, like it inevitably does between sisters. But that isn't how it was those first few weeks, and maybe that's because I'd just turned six, and the idea that one day your family looks one way and the next day it looks another way was all that I knew.

The years between then and now taught me the dangerous lesson that comfort and solace can be found in the everyday rhythms of a predictable life. The years in between taught me that you can rely on things to be a certain way when you wake up in the morning.

Now I know again that one day things can be going along like they always were and then, suddenly, in a simple rotation of an overheated planet, everything can change.

It's a hell of a lot harder to take this lesson at seventeen than it was at two. Or six.

But I'm getting ahead of myself.

Back to the day of the wedding and my white tulle dress with the splattered mud and electric-green grass stains.

It was perfect.

# HERE

F. Gregory has short dark hair that sticks up in just the right way and in just the right places. She has three earrings in one ear and two in the other. She's sporting the perfect pair of jeans.

I hate her.

No, I don't hate her. Of course I don't hate her. Let's be honest. She has the look I've always wanted but never even tried for because it's so far beyond my reach I'd dislocate something just attempting to graze it with my fingertips.

She's cool. I'm not, particularly.

I have long blond hair. It doesn't ever do a thing that would come close to approaching stylish. It's straight and flat and thin. It's blond, sure, and some people will tell you that it's a beautiful color, but they're lying. It's dull.

I don't have anything pierced because I'm a complete wuss when it comes to pain. If I could step into a world where the idea of somebody taking a gun and shooting some part of my flesh with a sharp metal stud didn't make me physically ill, I think I'd get a nose ring. A small diamond just above my left nostril. Something on my face that sparkles, that would make you want to look at me.

Also, I can't wear jeans.

This is a fact. I've tried. I even tried wearing the expensive kind of jeans. The upward-of-two-hundred-dollars kind. Well, they were two hundred and twenty-four dollars. After I wore them three times I had to admit that they didn't work on me.

I sold them on eBay.

For two hundred dollars.

So basically I spent twenty-four dollars plus postage and handling to learn something I already knew: that I can't wear jeans.

F. Gregory is wearing forty-dollar Levi's and they look fantastic.

Her plane arrived from New York. So we have something to talk about while we stand around waiting for S. JARVIS.

"Sue?" I ask Linus.

"Seth," he says. "I believe that places you in the wrong forty-nine-point-three percent."

"Damn."

F. Gregory's real name is Frances, and she lives in the West Village with her mom; her dad lives on the Upper East Side. My grandparents live on the Upper West Side and I have an uncle in the East Village, so between us we have the four corners of New York City fairly well covered.

I just tell her I live in Los Angeles and don't say anything else about whom I live with or where, and she doesn't ask, and I'm totally and completely relieved because I start to taste my pounding heart just thinking about how to answer any more questions. I sit down on my suitcase and start digging through my backpack like I'm looking for something, and she turns and starts talking to Linus, probably writing me off as a stuck-up bitch who's too cool to make polite conversation.

I don't really care.

I didn't come here to make friends. I came here to forget friends. And sort-of boyfriends. And sisters. And mothers.

○ ○ ○

Seth Jarvis has a buzz cut. He's from Salt Lake City and he's wearing khaki shorts, flip-flops and a baggy white T-shirt that doesn't quite mask his boy boobs. He's carrying a big bottle of water.

In the van, as we leave Memphis behind and I take one last longing look at civilization, Linus turns the radio to a country music station. Seth Jarvis seems to know the song that's playing. He and Linus discuss another version that Seth likes better.

I hate country music.

I hate country music so much that I considered *not* coming to Tennessee. Homes from the Heart has other summer programs for teens. There's one in Guatemala. But I haven't heard enough Guatemalan music to know if I hate it or not. And anyway, I knew about the tornado. I saw the picture of the boy with the tear running down his dusty face.

Disasters don't pass me by just because they're small.

There was an article about this tornado on the Web site I visit devoted to climate change. This scientist believes that tornadoes, hurricanes, tsunamis and fill-in-the-blank disasters are a direct result of global warming. They're caused by human activity. If we change the way we live our lives, he argues, we could decrease disaster in the world.

I've read plenty of the other types of articles too. The ones where the scientists argue that disasters are inevitable, that no matter what we do, there are certain disasters that will always befall us.

After a long drive we turn off the highway and spend another twenty-five minutes traversing smaller roads. I notice a pattern. It goes something like: church, church, fast-food restaurant I've never heard of, church, muffler shop, church, church.

We stop at an intersection.

"Downtown Bailey, people. Blink and you'll miss it." Linus takes his foot off the brake and we roll on. I look out the window behind me. Some storefronts. American flags. A woman with red hair sits on a bench.

In another few minutes we arrive at what Linus calls our hotel, though actually it's a motel on the side of an empty road. No restaurants or muffler shops. Not a single church. It sits alone. Even trees keep their distance.

I'm assigned to 7W, room 7 on the West Wing. Girls on the West Wing. Boys on the East Wing. By the way, calling the two sides of this place wings won't fill it with glamour.

But here's the thing.

I love it here.

As I turn the key in my door and step into the floral-polyester-curtained darkness, a smell wafts over me of a room that was once a place where you could smoke. I take in the tacky art on the walls, the moth-eaten orange armchair, a cracked mirror, and I fall in love.

It's a place of anonymity. A generic room that could be anywhere. It *is* anywhere, and it's nowhere, and for the next twelve weeks, it's a place I can call my own.

# HOME

Tess and Rose have a dad.

They have a dad who isn't my dad.

At first I found this really hard to take. When they moved into our house and we were a family and Jane was the mom and Dad was the dad, I took it as a personal affront every time Avi showed up to collect Tess and Rose. I pretended I didn't hear the doorbell.

If we didn't answer the door I thought maybe he'd go away.

*If a doorbell rings in your house and no one goes to answer it, do your sisters have a different father?*

I sulked. I moped. I did all the things kids do when they feel sorry for themselves.

Finally it was determined that it made more sense if, when Avi came to take his daughters, he just took all three of us.

I don't know whose idea this was, but it was brilliant.

I grew to love Avi.

I still do even though he's soon to become my ex-stepsisters' father or my ex-stepmother's ex-husband, and that may be too wide a gap for us to bridge. We were already nothing to each other, strictly speaking.

Avi lives at the beach.

When you walk in the front door of his apartment and you look across the living room to the glass sliding doors that lead out to the deck, for a minute all you can see is water, and it feels like you just stepped onto a boat.

When we were younger, we'd spend our Saturday nights there. Avi would order Chinese food. We'd rent movies. In the mornings we'd eat bagels sitting on the sand in our pajamas.

Avi's a writer. He writes for the *Los Angeles Times*.

Now when the paper comes to our house in the mornings, I skim it to see if he has a byline, and if he does, I fold the paper up and throw it in the recycling bin.


# HERE


Our first community meeting is tonight.

We're meeting by the pool. Our motel has a pool. Hooray.

I've got a few hours to kill so I decide to take a walk, but I only make it as far as the gas station up the road, where I go in and fight the urge to buy a real root beer. I reach for a diet Hines root beer in a can and I feel a pang for L.A. with all its fancy brands of microbrewed sodas in their designer bottles.

I stand inside the air-conditioned gas station mart and

watch the heat melting the asphalt road. It rises like a spirit. Like all the life is picking itself up off the surface of the earth in search of someplace better. Or at least cooler.

Even before arriving here, I spent a lot of my time thinking about heat. It's hard not to think about heat when the ten hottest years in recorded history have all occurred in my lifetime, and every shred of reliable science points to the earth only getting hotter. But I've never *seen* what heat actually looks like, until this empty asphalt road in the middle of nowhere.

When I walk back to the motel and open the door to room 7W I find a girl unpacking an enormous suitcase.

I didn't count on this.

This was my spot of anonymity. My place to be alone. *I don't know a soul.*

Yet I trip over someone else's shoes at my very own doorstep.

Apparently I have a roommate.

She has dark curly hair and thin, rectangular black glasses. Her shoes, the ones I tripped over at the door, are those outdoorsy, hiking-in-the-mountains-but-if-you-come-across-a-stream-you'll-be-okay-in-the-water kind of shoes.

"Oops. Sorry about that," she says as she grabs them and puts them in the closet. My closet. "I'm in the habit of taking off my shoes whenever I step inside anywhere. My mother is compulsive about her imported rugs."

I'm trying to readjust. I feel the quiet nights of lying in bed alone, staring at the ceiling, or maybe writing letters I'll never send, slipping away from me.

"I'm Marisol. My flight was late. There was a power outage at the San Francisco airport, which didn't do much to boost my confidence in the aviation industry."

"I'm Harper."

I try to seem upbeat, happy to meet her, thrilled to find her unpacking, but I don't think I'm doing a very good job.

The best I can come up with is to offer her some of my diet Hines root beer in a can. She takes a pass.

"Where are you from?" she asks.

"Los Angeles," I say, and then I go into the bathroom and shut the door behind me even though I have no business to take care of in there. I turn on the faucet and let it run for a minute. Then I feel guilty about wasting water.

It's a paradox. The polar ice caps are melting. The oceans are rising. A terrifying future of too much water looms ahead of us, yet water is something we're constantly told we need to conserve. It's a precious resource. It's precious and yet there's a very real threat posed by having too much of it.

I'm pretty sure that's a paradox.

I splash some water on my face, dry it with a threadbare towel and come out of the bathroom to try again with Marisol.

"It's hot as hell here," I say, and as soon as I do, I notice a crucifix around her neck. "Oh, damn." My hand flies up to cover my mouth. "Oh my God. I said *damn*. Sorry for that.

And for the *hell*. And while I'm at it, I guess I should apologize for the *God* too."

She looks at me like I'm completely insane.

I gesture to her neck.

"Oh please." She worries the crucifix between her fingers. "I swear like a sailor. Honestly. It makes my mother crazy. She's from Mexico. She doesn't speak much English, but she knows the four-letter words. I try, but it's like the more I think about cleaning up my language, the dirtier it gets. It's my one vice. That and caffeine."

"That's two." I wish I hadn't just said that. I have this habit of being annoyingly particular and literal about language.

She smiles and takes off her glasses, cleaning the lenses with her tank top. "So it is."

We walk together to our first community meeting, because that's what roommates do. They stick together. Everyone is flocking to the pool in pairs, like various species on our way to the ark.

We sit on lounge chairs missing vinyl straps. I do a quick count. There are sixteen of us. An even mix of boys and girls. I wonder who they are and why they're here. Are they running from something? Did they see a heartbreaking photograph?

Linus is wearing a white T-shirt and his arms are covered with a forest of red hair. He's sitting on the concrete with his back to the pool and his legs folded underneath him.

His eyes are closed.

People are starting to get uncomfortable now, waiting for him to acknowledge that we've arrived for the meeting, but he's still sitting there with closed eyes, his chest rising and falling with slow, deep breaths.

I guess by people, I really mean me. *I'm* getting uncomfortable now. I feel like I'm witnessing a private moment, but I can't seem to take my eyes off him. He looks like he's meditating, which seems weird because from what little I know of lumberjacks they aren't the meditating kind. They're big and strong and simple, if they even exist at all and aren't just made up to sell paper towels.

Finally someone says, loudly, "Dude. What's up?"

Linus opens his eyes and smiles. He stands and stretches. He takes a deep breath and clasps his hands together.

"Welcome. It's a blessing to have you all here, gathered in this beautiful place. Over the next twelve weeks, we will learn the value of togetherness, what happens when we get together, when we open ourselves up to one another, and to the greater community beyond. I hope what we find is that with two hands you can do divine work, without limitation, as if you had an infinite number of hands."

All I can think about while he's talking is, *I'm going to kill Dad.*

All I knew was that I wanted to help that boy in the picture, the one with the tear on his dusty face. It was Dad who found the Homes from the Heart Summer Program for Teens. I could go spend the summer building a house, he said. It's a great program, he said, and it's one of the few teen volunteer programs not affiliated with any religious institution. Or cult. He said.

I take a quick look around to catch someone's eye for a quick eye roll, a shared moment of understanding about how weird this guy is, but then I realize that those eye rolls only work with people you know and who know you back.

"How many of you have ever built anything?" Linus asks.

That's a reasonable question, so I begin to consider it.

At home on the living room rug: Lego towers, Lincoln Log cabins. At school: dinosaur dioramas, Popsicle-stick bridges.

This probably isn't what he's after, so I don't raise my hand.

I'm the only one who doesn't.

So, naturally, the next word out of Linus's mouth is "Harper." He looks at me and smiles. "You've never built a thing?"

"Not really."

"Nothing?"

"Nothing other than kid stuff."

"What about friendships?" He scratches his beard. "Dreams? Plans for your future?"

"Well, yeah, sure, but . . ."

"Then you're prepared. You already have the important tools. I'm just going to introduce you to a few new ones like a leveler and a circular saw. Simple stuff." He scans the rest of the group. "We'll start with all that tomorrow, okay? Tonight your work is to get to know each other."

Other employees of Homes from the Heart arrive with trays of food and buckets of bottled water and soda. I watch as everyone sizes up everyone else. We're all we've got for the next twelve weeks.

There are a few kids who've done this program before, but most of us are here for the first time. There's a lot of talk about wanting to do something that matters, rather than teaching campers how to weave a proper lanyard. A few kids are genuinely interested in learning carpentry skills. One boy says his father thought this experience would teach him how to be a man.

There's a beautiful Japanese girl named Marika with hair to the small of her back and the body of a ballerina.

"You mean we have to work?" she deadpans. "I thought this was a performing arts camp."

Dessert is served, and even though it's turned dark and the moon sits low in the sky, the Popsicles start melting the minute the wrappers come off. I soak up as many details about everybody as I can without giving too much of myself away.

There are sounds all around me. Noises I've never heard. A symphony of Tennessee insects humming in the darkness.

And then I go back to my room, and I sleep facing the wall, and I try my best to pretend that I'm alone.

## HOME

I dream of Gabriel.

I wish to God I didn't.

I met Gabriel in sixth grade when both of our elementary schools fed into the same middle school. Seated next to me in Mr. Ratner's math class, he became my first friend who also happened to be a boy.

It's not as if I didn't know boys growing up. There were boys on my street and boys whose parents were friends of Dad and Jane. But Gabriel was my first friend who also happened to be a boy with whom I talked on the phone and went to the movies, or just hung around the house complaining about how there's nothing to do when you're too young to drive in L.A.

Gabriel wasn't always so serious. He once read comic books. He perfected a dead-on imitation of the lunch lady. He'd put his hands over his head and jiggle his hips and bare his stomach like a belly dancer. It was his good-luck dance, performed in the moments when he needed some luck, like when he dialed our local radio station, praying that he'd be caller ninety-four, so we could score free tickets to the Green Day concert.

This was all before I grew breasts and he grew six inches.

Cheekbones pushed their way out of his doughy boy cheeks. His eyes sank in a little deeper and green flecks appeared out of nowhere.

One night when he was over and we were watching a DVD, I was lying with my head near his lap, and the arm he'd draped over the back of the couch slipped and grazed my newly grown breasts, and something started buzzing in me in a place I hardly knew existed.

He quickly picked up his arm and draped it back over the couch.

A few minutes passed. Then he gently picked up his arm, and lowered his hand purposefully onto my breast and left it there.

I stopped breathing.

We were still. We didn't move an inch.

Then, slowly, I arched my back and pushed against his hand, and he grabbed me harder, and I let out a mortifying moan.

We heard the key in the front door and I sat up. Panic crashing through me like a dropped stack of dishes.

Dad and Jane.

When the movie with a title that to this day I can't recall ended, Dad drove Gabriel home. We were only fourteen.

We didn't speak after that for a month.

Eventually we found our way back to each other, but without any honest conversation, or confession about true feelings, like you see on TV. One day we just started talking again as if there hadn't been this month of silence, or the hand-to-breast contact, between us.

We went back to being friends for two more years. I'd help him shop for clothes. He'd burn me CDs. I'd read his English papers. We developed an addiction to blueberry-banana smoothies from a stand near the beach.

During that time he had many girlfriends, not just friends who happened to be girls, but girlfriends who also noticed his cheekbones and green-flecked eyes. Girlfriends he took to school dances and parties on nights I'd hang out with Tess and pretend I didn't care.

Did I care?

I don't even know how to answer that. Something resembling jealousy gnawed at me, but I don't know if that was because of Gabriel's interest in other girls, or because those girls basked in the warm light of a boy's interest. It made them walk taller. Heads high. Chests out. Smiles adorably coy.

Gabriel became somebody who probably wouldn't have given me the time of day if we hadn't become friends early on. He became the boy all the girls talked about. Quiet, serious, cool Gabriel. And I was the girl who could approach him at school without getting tongue-tied, the girl everyone knew was Gabriel's old friend Harper, who nobody envied, because nobody wanted to be the girl he saw, with those beautiful green-flecked eyes, as just a friend.

And then, finally, someone else started to notice me, it doesn't really matter who, it was just a boy who wasn't Gabriel, and it was only then that Gabriel showed his interest in me again.

## HERE

There's a knock at our door at six-thirty a.m.

I hear Linus's booming voice. "C'mon, everyone. Breakfast is in half an hour. Don't be late. We need every single one of you beautiful people."

He's moving his way down the West Wing, pounding on every door.

Does this place have any other guests? If it does, how do they feel about Linus shouting about breakfast, as if it's the apocalypse, at six-thirty in the morning?

I roll over and look across the room. Marisol's bed is empty. As I adjust my eyes to the light, and this wonderfully dingy, anonymous room, I realize that the shower is running.

Marisol and I go to breakfast together, a spread of donuts and muffins and little boxes of low-rent cereals with too much sugar. I grab a banana and a cup of coffee that comes out looking like filthy tap water.

*Starbucks. Peet's. Coffee Bean & Tea Leaf.*

I find myself whispering the names of the places at home, on every corner, where I could find a cup of coffee worth getting up at six-thirty for.

Everyone seems excited. They're freshly showered. Dressed in tank tops and lace-up work boots. Hats emblazoned with the names of sports teams or local restaurants or vacation destinations on their heads.

The room smells of sunblock.

There's a palpable buzz in the air. And I can say with absolute certainty, it isn't from the coffee.

My stomach is unsettled. My banana is barely going down. I'm tired, sure, and wondering what it is I'm doing here with all these strangers in the conference room of a motel in the middle of nowhere, sitting in a folding chair drinking crappy coffee. But I also have that first-day-of-school feeling.

That delicious mix of anticipation and dread.

Linus comes in carrying a cardboard box filled with spiral notebooks. He begins to pass them around. They have our names on them. I start to open mine but then Linus is standing on a folding chair yelling about how there's time for reading about what we're doing later. Now it's time to start *doing* what we're doing.

"Here's what you need to know: we're going to do right by this family. They deserve it. Since April they've done nothing but help clean up their neighbors' houses while their own lies in ruins. Those neighbors wrote to us on their behalf. They asked us to come and help and that's what we're here to do. We're going to give this family something better, something safer than what they had before. You don't know it yet, but you can do it. There're some other teams down here working on some other houses, but you're the only teenage group, and you're the only ones who've given your entire summer over to this project. We're going to prove that you can do this job better than anybody else. Now let's get to it."

He herds us all outside. The bus is spewing thick black smoke into the already scorching-hot air around us and I start to do some impossible calculation in my head about whether the bad by-products of trying to do good (individual cereal boxes, foam coffee cups, gas-guzzling buses) outweigh the good deeds themselves.

I get nowhere.

Marisol and I sit together. Roommates cling to each other like life rafts.

She does most of the talking. She's into hiking and camping, which explains her hideous shoes.

"I can't relate," I say. "Why sleep on the ground when there are beds? Why walk when you could drive?"

"You're so L.A."

"And you're so smug. Typical Northern Californian."

She laughs. "I'll take you camping sometime. I'll convert you."

"Please don't."

"So what brings you here?"

"You go first."

"Well, my mom wanted me to go on a trip with my church youth group this summer. Of course. And I convinced her to let me come here by promising to go to church every Sunday, but I just don't see that happening."

"You have plenty to choose from in these parts."

"I noticed. But I think I'll work on learning how to sleep late instead."

"I'm a bit of a sleep expert. So if you need some coaching, look no further."

"Excellent," she says, and readjusts her glasses. "Mom used to do missionary work, both my parents did, so they were pretty psyched about this program, but I think they were just as psyched that I'd be getting away from Pierre. He's my boyfriend. He's almost twenty. That they're not so psyched about. They still think I'm eight."

I start to tell her a little about why I wanted to come, how Dad found this program for me. I tell her about wanting to help, and less about wanting to run away, but I do say something about how things at home are a mess.

Then we fall silent. Most of the bus does. Struck dumb by what we see outside our windows.

Houses with their roofs torn off. Barns lying on their sides. Piles and piles of wood and insulation mixed up with unrecognizable appliance parts, furniture stuffing, panes of glass and the bright primary-colored plastic of toys.

In fact, the houses and the barns look sort of like toys, knocked over by one gigantic, clumsy toddler.

And in between are stretches of quiet, idyllic countryside that take on an eerie quality. Like in a horror movie when you know that too much quiet means something evil is lurking, a long stretch of green starts to hint that a new pile of wreckage can't be too far off.

"This is it, people," Linus says in a voice without its boom. "The path of the tornado."

We pull off a dirt road into a big parking lot surrounded by about a dozen trailers. When we file out I take in a deep breath of the dust kicked up by the bus and some of the lingering exhaust.

I feel the heat through my clothes. On the crown of my uncovered head. I reach into my bag and pull out an L.A. Dodgers cap.

"Over here, campers," Linus calls from the shade of a tree.

The trailers are lived-in. You can tell by the chairs clustered around barbecues. Soccer balls. Plastic kiddie pools. Shoes lined up outside front doors. Laundry hanging from ropes tied between the trailers' roofs. But there aren't many people standing outside, and I suspect that this has something to do with the heat.

We gather around Linus, clutching our water bottles.

He does a head count and then turns and starts walking. We exchange some puzzled looks and follow. I'm next to the guy who snapped Linus out of his meditative stupor last night. He's pretty cute. We exchange a look, my first shared moment of understanding since I arrived here.

He's got shaggy blond hair and a deep tan. He obviously didn't read the instructions about what to wear to work, or else he chose to ignore them, because he's got worn-out flip-flops on his brown feet.

We walk for what feels like a long time. The air is so thick it's like wading through water. The land is flat. The grass is dried out and brittle and it crackles beneath my boots.

A single bird flies in a slow, lazy loop above us.

Finally we come to a large stretch of caramel-colored dirt flattened by some kind of truck or tractor.

Linus reaches down and begins to unlace his boots. In the distance I can see more wreckage. A pile of chaos.

"Shoes off," he says.

I'm thinking that cute blond tan boy had some information I didn't as I watch him slip right out of his sandals. I begin the long process of unlacing my heavy boots.

"Sit in a circle," Linus says, and he waits as we arrange ourselves.

"By the time you leave here and go back to your lives,

your friends, your family and your schoolwork, by the time our twelve weeks together is up, there will be a house. Right here where we sit."

I take a look around. It's pretty hard to imagine that a house will be standing here so fast.

Some kind of bug lands on my foot and I take a swipe at it and I wonder what on earth Linus was thinking, having us remove our shoes out here.

"This is sacred ground," he says.

I look up at the empty sky. The bird is gone.

"This is going to be somebody's home. Treat it with respect. Home is a sacred place."

# STEP TWO:

# LAY THE FOUNDATION

They moved out in October.

Even though Tess and I stopped sharing a room after Rose left for college, when Tess moved out of our house, somehow my room felt empty.

I tried rearranging the furniture.

Desk by the window. Bed in the corner.

I put new posters on the walls. I covered practically every square inch of the sea-green paint.

Nothing worked.

Here's something it's important to know about Tess: she's my best friend.

Or at least she was. It's all pretty unclear now.

She was my sister.

Now she isn't.

That is crystal clear.

# HERE

Linus gives out our assignments. He puts us in pairs, or what he calls our double-y partnerships, the double y standing for—are you ready for this—yin and yang.

But I quickly forgive Linus when he informs me that my double-y partner for the week is that cute shaggy blond boy.

His name is Captain, which apparently is not a nickname, but *his actual legal name*. I even check his driver's license, and there it is.

Captain and I spend the day digging holes for the footing, which I now know is one of the first steps in laying the foundation of a house.

The house will be a rectangle, forty by sixty feet with a front porch and a set of steps from the kitchen in the back. The plans are in our notebook. A dizzying array of diagrams, measurements and terminology, as incomprehensible to me as if they were in Arabic. But flipping through the pages during a much-needed break from digging, I notice something.

"There's no basement," I say to Linus as he comes by to check on our progress. "Why?"

"Too expensive."

"But where are these people supposed to go if there's ever another tornado? Where do they hide?"

"There's a shortcut for everything, and in this case it's called a tornado-safe room. We buy it prefab and install it inside the house. No doubt it'd be better and safer to have a basement, but our budget simply doesn't allow it."

I look up and see that Captain has wandered over to Seth and Frances, who are putting wooden stakes in the dirt and then connecting them with bright pink plastic roll tape. Captain has taken some of the tape and tied his hair into pigtails with big pink plastic bows.

I nod in Captain's direction. "Yeah. I can only imagine how tight your budget must be if we're who you're counting on to get this house built."

Linus laughs and then he looks me in the eye. "You're here because you want to be here, all of you. And that, Harper, is priceless." He walks away.

Have I mentioned the heat?

There should be another word for what it feels like out here in the sun, because *hot* is coming up seriously short. I have big sweat stains under my arms like our sixty-year-old Russian next-door neighbor, Mr. Sidorov.

By the end of the day I've dug four holes. When we get back to the motel I'm exhausted, a little sunburned, and my body hurts all over.

There's a barbecue going on out by the pool. Hamburgers and hot dogs and potato salad. Limp American cheese in plastic wrap, the kind we were never allowed at home.

I'm sitting with my feet in the hot tub, next to Captain,

who, I'm happy to report, has removed his pigtails. His legs are muscular and he has a scar on his left knee. I find myself wanting to run my finger along it, but don't, of course.

I'm not sure what's come over me. The humidity, maybe. One day of hard work in the heat and I seem to have forgotten my vow of solitude. My legs are on fire from the sunburn, but I sit here with my feet dangling in the too-hot water listening to Captain talk.

He's from Florida, which explains the tan. He has some family who lost their home in a hurricane when he was seven, which explains why he's here. He just broke up with his girl-friend of a year, which explains why I'm sitting next to him, and why, under the bubbling water, I just grazed his foot with my own.

Her name is Marcy. He says she never understood him.

*I understand you*, I think, even though I also understand that I don't know this guy at all. One shared puzzled look and a day of digging holes in the sun and I've lost all perspective.

But then I think about where knowing somebody has got-ten me: nowhere. No, someplace worse than nowhere, be-cause when you're nowhere I'm pretty sure you feel nothing.

Maybe this is just what I need. I need to *not* know some-body. I've known Gabriel since sixth grade. I know everything about him.

I take my feet out of the water and fold them underneath me. "If you want my opinion, understanding someone, or know-ing someone, or whatever you want to call it, is way overrated."

"What do you mean?"

"I mean it doesn't really matter how well you know somebody, it doesn't make love any easier, it might just make it harder."

He smiles a big broad smile at me that's almost as beautiful as the last light of this fading summer night.

"Yeah, you're probably right," he says, and then his look turns conspiratorial. "Listen. There's some talk of a midnight swim. You in?"

*That's against the rules.*

Oops—I said that out loud. I didn't mean to do that. I'm a stickler for rules, but that's not one of the first things I like someone knowing about me.

"It's going to be a long twelve weeks with that kind of attitude."

"Okay," I say. "Count me in." My sunburn has turned from a feeling that my skin is too tight for my body into a wonderful tingling feeling of skin that is suddenly alive.

"Awesome." And then, because things always seem to end up this way when it comes to me and boys, he adds: "You know Frances, right? Wanna check with her? See if she wants to come too?"

This should make me feel sorry for myself, but somehow it doesn't. Of course Captain likes Frances. Who wouldn't? Just look at her. She's standing on the other side of the pool talking to Seth, probably about music, with one earbud of his iPod in her ear, and she's moving, slightly, but unmistakably, to the rhythm of hip-hop. Poor Seth. He doesn't know yet that he doesn't stand a chance.

I know why I'm here. I'm here to work and to forget and I don't need any complications in the form of Captain, even if just a minute ago it was what I thought I needed.

We'll be friends. Just friends who are not anything more. He will be a real boy friend.

It feels like a relief.

I reach out my finger and touch his scar and I ask him how he got it and when he tells me that he fell off his skateboard, I know something new about my friend Captain.

And when midnight rolls around, I stay in bed and watch as the red numbers on my digital alarm clock continue to flick by.

# HOME

The last Thanksgiving before they moved out, we ate dinner at midnight. Jane had to work late, and the idea of having Thanksgiving without her was unthinkable.

So we invited our guests for a midnight meal, when the whole family could be together.

The Berkows and the Feldmans came, like they do every year. And Avi came too, with his new girlfriend, Lynn. We woke up Cole when all the food was spread out, and he ate his meal in his pajamas with the race cars on them, a streak of dried toothpaste still on his chin.

Tess and I made everything: sweet potatoes with melted marshmallows on top, creamed spinach, fresh cranberry sauce, roasted asparagus. Neither of us had ever done much cooking, so we were a little overwhelmed by this sixteen-pound bird with no head. We stood there in the kitchen that afternoon, staring it down.

"Cole was only eight pounds at birth," said Tess, cocking her head. She was wearing a blue plaid apron and holding a wooden spoon as if it were a weapon. She leaned in closer to the turkey. "We probably could have fit him inside this thing."

"And he might have tasted better than the stuffing recipe you picked. Artichoke hearts? In stuffing? Vomit."

It was excellent. And so was the turkey when we took it from the oven at eleven p.m. Golden brown without the dry stringy parts I remembered from all the Thanksgivings before. It tasted even better because Tess and I did it together without any help from anyone.

Something felt glamorous about the night. Magical. While all the houses in the neighborhood were dark, while everyone else crawled into bed with too-full stomachs, our holiday was just beginning.

Our guests didn't leave until the sun started to come up. We walked them to the door and watched as Avi and Lynn had to dodge the early-morning sprinklers of our next-door neighbor's front lawn to reach their car.

We vowed to make this a tradition.

We'd have Thanksgiving at midnight every year, no matter what. A magical midnight Thanksgiving.

But this past year, the very next Thanksgiving, it was just Dad and me. Cole was with Jane and Tess, and Rose, who'd come home for the weekend. I don't know what they did or when they ate or who cooked the turkey.

Dad and I went out for Thai food and were home in bed by ten.

# HERE

I'm starting to realize that every place comes with its own ubiquitous noise.

In Los Angeles, it's lawn mowers. In New York City, it's cabdrivers abusing their horns.

In Bailey, Tennessee, it's bugs.

The air is always humming. You can even hear it over the sound of power tools.

By the third morning at the site, I start to think I've developed a sleepwalking habit. I must be waking in the night, going to the middle of the interstate, lying down and letting the eighteen-wheeled semis en route from Nashville to Memphis run over my body, one after the other. The two little Advils Linus doled out at breakfast looked like a joke in the palm of his hand. Nothing that small could do anything for a pain this big.

But I'm here.

There are all kinds of people here, which comes as a relief. We're a pretty solid bunch of kids. We want to do good. But there's no way we can do this on our own.

So I'm thrilled to see plumbers, electricians and guys in orange hard hats with the keys to the heavy machinery.

There're other volunteers. A bunch of big burly guys wearing Bailey High Football T-shirts. There's a woman, too old to even be out in the heat if you ask me, passing out fresh limeade in plastic cups.

There's a huge mountain of gravel today that seems to have risen out of thin air. Seth and Frances and Marisol and her partner, Lana, are removing the gravel from the pile and raking it around the low cement-block walls of the foundation we put up yesterday.

Captain and I are cutting wood.

Linus gave us a lesson this morning on the ins and outs of a worm-drive saw, how we're simply to guide it and let it do all the work.

"It knows what it needs to do," he tells us, and with that, another look passes between Captain and me.

But then the wood vibrates beneath my gloves as it slides under the saw and breaks in two, and one end of it falls to the earth with a *ka-thump*. It's pretty cool.

We stop for lunch. So far it's been a brown paper bag with a slightly soggy sandwich, a tired piece of fruit and no-name potato chips.

Today there's a table with a spread of ribs, roasted corn, a green salad and a vase of wildflowers. A tall woman with pale, freckled skin and thick blond braids is standing proudly behind it, serving spoon in hand. Diane Wright. It's her house we're building. This is a thank-you buffet lunch.

"Come and get it, y'all," she says, complete with Southern twang. She's the kind of woman you want to let hug you.

Wide smile and wider bosom. She's got a frilly apron and everything.

We eat, and I keep myself from hitting the buffet for the third time. I didn't realize the true vileness of our poolside dinner cookouts until my first taste of Diane's ribs.

Her family walks up from the trailers where they've been living since April. There's her husband, Wesley, an inch or two shorter than Diane, with rich black skin, a salt-and-pepper beard and wire-rimmed glasses. They have nine-year-old twins, Alice and Grace, indistinguishable except that one wears a white summer dress and the other wears cutoff jeans shorts. The one in the dress takes a seat next to me on the grass and ties a pile of dandelions into a long necklace.

The son, Teddy, looks to be my age. His skin is the color of a latte, dotted randomly with some of his mother's freckles, and his hair is cropped in tight curls close to his head. He's tall and painfully skinny, with a crooked smile and deep dimples. He wears baggy skater shorts and a T-shirt from a blues club in Memphis.

As we sit in the shade, lazy with the heat and richness of Diane's food, not too far from where their house once stood, they tell us about the tornado.

After, they thought about leaving. Going somewhere far away. But this is home. People needed them here. Diane is a nurse and the only doctor in Bailey had moved his family to Atlanta.

Tornadoes don't have names like hurricanes do. But they should.

It doesn't seem right that this thing came here and did what it did to these houses and farms and these lives—people living in trailers, some people not living at all—and yet this thing doesn't have a name by which we can call it.

And curse it.

While Wesley is talking, the twin in the shorts climbs into Teddy's lap and he takes her hair in his hands and twists it.

My insides ache.

My body feels like it wants to cave in on itself, and it isn't because this family has lost everything. It's because of the little girl sitting in her brother's lap and the way he holds her hair, and the dandelion necklace, and Wesley's protective arm around Diane's pale, freckled shoulder.

I ache, not for what they don't have.

I ache for what they do have.

## HOME

When I saw Tess at school the first Monday after they'd moved out, she was wearing a shirt I'd never seen.

That might not sound like such a big deal, but it was. Tess and I always did all our shopping together.

I favor long-sleeved T-shirts over tank tops. Cords or cargo pants. Black Vans. Occasionally, a denim skirt.

Tess is more fashionable. More feminine. Her shirts are always a little tighter and her shoes more delicate.

This shirt Tess wore was light pink and had snaps down the front that stopped right below her chest, and underneath she had on a gray ribbed tank top we'd bought together over the summer at this store on the Promenade. When Tess walked out of the dressing room, her long curly hair falling over her shoulders, the gray of the tank top somehow deepening the green in her eyes, she looked like a model. People in the store stopped to stare.

"What do you think?" she asked.

I lied. "You look okay."

I turned and poked through a rack of on-sale summer skirts.

In the hallway at school I said, "I like your new shirt. It looks amazing on you."

"Thanks," she said, and we went to our next classes.

Everything had changed, and I'm not just talking about Dad and Jane. Or Tess moving out. Or how Cole would become my part-time little brother.

There was more.

Dad told me on a Thursday night. I'll probably always question their decision to tell us separately.

I'd stayed after school for an environmental club meeting. When I got home, the house was quiet. Cole was in bed. Dad was in the kitchen alone.

"Where are Jane and Tess?"

"Out."

If I hadn't been so wrapped up in the argument we'd had over Alternative Energy Awareness Day, I might have noticed that Dad said "out" as if it took every ounce of life left in him to utter that one syllable. But it's only because I know what came after that word that I can go back and attach meaning to the way it was spoken.

Dad at the counter. An empty Scotch glass with two almost-melted cubes of ice. A pad of paper with some sort of list scratched in Dad's illegible scrawl. An unwashed dish in the sink.

Me, standing in front of the refrigerator. A bottle of Hank's root beer to my lips. The agenda from my meeting, folded, in my other hand.

Then he said it.

"We're getting a divorce."

That would be when I dropped everything.

Remarkably, the bottle didn't break.

In all the detail I remember about that moment, from Dad's melting ice cubes to the sound of the soda glug-glugging out of the dropped glass bottle, I can scarcely remember anything that came after.

But here's what I do know.

Here's what I know that made the newness of Tess's pink snap shirt insignificant, even though Tess shopping without me violated an unspoken rule of our sisterhood. As I stood there facing her that Monday morning after, and I told her that I liked her shirt, I was facing her with a secret.

Tess and I never kept secrets from each other.

Dad told me on a Thursday. Jane and Tess were at that very moment in a new house. I learned later that Jane had signed a lease on it a month before, and she had spent the weeks in between preparing for the move. By Friday night, Cole was there too.

On Saturday night, after years of imagining it, but knowing it should never happen, I did something neither Tess nor I had ever done.

I had sex.

With Gabriel.

# HERE

I've been in Tennessee a week now. It's Sunday and I'm supposed to call Dad.

Every Sunday. That's our deal.

I've never gone a whole week without talking to Dad. And it feels like it's been longer. That conversation on Linus's cell phone in the heat outside the airport feels like it took place a lifetime ago between Dad and some other version of me.

I'm not trying to say I've been transformed. That spending a week in Tennessee on a construction site has made me a better, more evolved, selfless person who isn't wrapped up in her own problems. Or that I'm suddenly confident. Strong. Able to erect new homes in a single bound.

It's just that Dad and the sound of his voice feel very far away.

Yesterday was our first day off.

When I woke up at eleven o'clock, sweet, sweet eleven

o'clock, I found most of the group out by the pool. What I saw when I looked around provided a tidy summation of our first week together.

1. Captain was rubbing sunblock onto Frances's lower back.

2. Seth was sitting on the edge of Marika's lounge chair, scrolling through his iPod picking out a song for her to listen to, while pretending he wasn't checking out her string bikini. And she, kindly, pretended not to notice that he wouldn't, despite the heat, remove his baggy white T-shirt and expose his boy boobs to the group.

3. Jared and Stacey, the first official couple of the summer, were in the pool. Their union became official, at least publicly so, when Linus threw open the door to the conference room after dinner Wednesday and found Stacey wrapped around Jared on one of the uncomfortable metal folding chairs.

(Technically, Jared and Stacey weren't breaking any rules when Linus found them. The rules say when you have to be in your own room and who can and cannot be in there with you. Nothing about conference rooms.)

Luckily, the social scene here isn't entirely about couples. Take my fourth observation:

4. Marisol was sitting with Lana and her sister, Jo, already known as the Chicago Sisters, playing a game of Scrabble.

They let me join in.

In some universes you'd look like a total geek sitting by the pool playing Scrabble. But it doesn't seem to matter here.

That evening the bus took us to a movie at a gigantic mall forty minutes away. I ate dinner with Marisol and Captain and Frances in the food court.

Frances had never eaten a meal in a mall in her life. "We don't really have malls in the city."

"The city," said Captain. "Why does everybody from New York call it the city, as if it's the only city in the entire world?"

"Because it's the only one that matters," said Frances.

Captain rolled his eyes.

I sat eating my salty french fries, thinking they had a very strange way of flirting with each other.

"So what brings you here?" I asked Frances. "To this mega-mall with really bad french fries in the middle of nowhere?"

"Just because I think New York is a superior place to live doesn't mean I don't care about what happens in the rest of the country." Then she got a sheepish look on her face. "And my guidance counselor said it would help me get into Brown."

"Ah, the truth," said Captain. "She's just as selfish and self-centered as your average dweller in the city."

After we got back, and after lights-out, I heard doors creaking open and flip-flops on their way for another midnight swim. I heard Captain and Frances giggling in the hallway.

"Are you going?" I asked Marisol. She was lying in her bed across the room reading a book in Spanish that looked like it weighed fifty pounds.

"No. I'm not looking to hook up, so better to get my beauty sleep. What about you?"

"Well, now you've set me up. If I say I want to go, I'm saying I want to hook up."

"By all means, don't let me stop you from reaching your full slut potential. Why shouldn't you? You're not a nice Catholic girl like me." She held up her crucifix.

"No, I'm not. But also I'm not looking for any more drama in my life. Anyway, I want to hear more about Pierre."

Stories about a real boyfriend who writes you letters and misses you when you're gone for the summer are as foreign to me as whatever was happening between the covers of Marisol's Spanish novel.

We stayed up talking until two a.m.

And then this morning I wake up at eleven, and the first thing I think is that either Marisol succumbed to her guilt and went off to church, or else she failed miserably in her first attempt to sleep late, because she's nowhere to be seen.

The second thing I think is that I have to call Dad.

He gave me a phone card that I shoved somewhere in my backpack. A phone card. It seems so quaint in the age of cell phones. When I go to dig for it, I feel something in the inside zippered pocket.

Oh, right. Dad. He told me about the thing in the inside zippered pocket.

Actually, it's two things.

I can tell before I pull it out what the first one is. A picture in a frame. Dad and Cole. Cole is sitting on Dad's lap, squinting at the camera, a Hot Wheels car in his hand. Pavlov lies next to them, his head resting on his black and white paws.

Before Cole was born, Dad liked to joke that in his house every night was Ladies' Night. We outnumbered him four to one. He'd complain about the suffocating levels of estrogen, but we all knew he loved every minute of it.

Now I'm outnumbered three to one, if you count a border collie as a boy.

I take the picture and hold it close to my face to see it more clearly in this dark room. You couldn't even tell where it was taken if you hadn't been there. But I took the picture with my new digital camera, out in the backyard at the end of last summer, in front of the lavender bushes, about six weeks before Dad and Jane split up.

I'd been experimenting with close-ups. How to get a tight shot without the subjects going blurry. It worked. Dad and Cole and Pavlov fill up the frame, sharp and crisp, but when I look at this picture, I see little other than the small empty spaces at its edges.

I put it next to my bed on the table with the wobbly leg.

The other thing I find in my backpack is a bag of jelly beans.

When I was little, I hated when Dad had to go away. All kids hate when their parents go away, but I *really* hated it. Maybe you could even call it a phobia. I was terrified that something would happen to him, and I guess you don't have to be Sigmund Freud to figure out where that came from.

So Dad would put one jelly bean into a little heart-shaped box for every night he'd be away. I'd eat one before bed, taking my time to choose just the right flavor, and think of him. And as they disappeared night after night, and I'd see how few were left, I'd know he'd be coming home soon.

I'm already a week behind on my jelly bean consumption, so I grab a handful and shove them in my mouth. It's a better way to start the morning than with a cup of motel coffee.

The phone rings five times before Dad picks up.

It's one of his weekends with Cole. Sunday-morning cartoons scream out from the background.

"Hey, honey!"

Dad sounds chipper. About one thousand times bigger than he did when I talked to him from the airport.

This makes me feel small. I'm standing out in the hallway, at the only pay phone, with no shoes on my feet and some serious bed-head.

"Hey," I say.

"How's Tennessee?"

"Hot."

"Yeah, I bet. I don't want to rub it in, but it is gorgeous here. Coley and I are thinking about hitting the beach. He's got a new boogie board."

Cole can barely swim.

Dad knows I'm a worrier, so he adds, "He likes to lie on it in the sand and have me drag him around."

"Sounds like fun."

"So, tell me more. What are you up to? Do you have friends? Will you be able to build me some shelves in my office when you get home?"

I'm alone. Maybe I slept too late. I don't see anyone hanging around. This is how I wanted it. I was hoping for some privacy. I didn't want to call home within earshot of anybody else.

"C'mon, Harper. Tell me something. Anything. Please?"

I tell him about the tornado. Its crazy path through this quiet countryside. The wrecked homes, and how some families just packed up and left. They gave up. I tell him about the Wrights, Diane and Wesley and the beautiful twins and skinny Teddy.

I tell him about how they stayed.

# HERE

On Monday Teddy's working at the site.

Homes from the Heart has a policy. If they come to build you a house, and they provide all these materials and all these laborers, even if the laborers are a bunch of teenagers, some of us quite lazy, you still have to help out. Which makes total sense. And since Diane runs the medical clinic and Wesley teaches summer school and the twins are only nine, the Wright family contribution falls to Teddy.

Teddy is my double-y partner for the week, and I'm missing Captain. I tried arguing with Linus. I told him what I learned in my Eastern philosophy elective last spring: that the yin is the dark, feminine, passive force and the yang is the bright, active, masculine force, and if he really knew anything about yin and yang he would know not only that Captain is the perfect yang to my yin, but also that it takes time for the two sides to figure out their roles, to really know each other's strengths and weaknesses, and tearing us apart right now is counterproductive.

Linus was unmoved.

When Captain and I worked together we talked all day long. He talked to me about Marcy and Frances. I told him about Gabriel, making our relationship sound much more official or simple or real than it ever was, because here in Tennessee, sixteen hundred miles from home, I can make it anything I want it to be.

He didn't ask me anything about my family.

Yin and yang. Perfect.

For the first hour, Teddy doesn't say a word, which is just as well, because even though I don't know him at all, I'm irritated with him for the simple reason that he's not Captain.

He listens to an MP3 player that is not an iPod, which I'm pretty sure puts him in violation of a rule. Okay, so maybe it strictly states no iPods at the construction site, but as I mentioned, I'm a stickler. The spirit of the rule is that you aren't supposed to have any kind of electronic listening device while working.

Maybe this is for safety purposes. Or to make sure we

communicate and get to know each other better. In that case, I think it's a stupid rule. You can't force people to talk to each other if they aren't interested. So, good for Teddy.

Sometime into the second hour Teddy takes out his earphones and puts his player into the pocket of his baggy shorts and he tilts back his baseball cap and he checks me out.

"Harper, right?"

"Yeah."

"Sorry for the antisocial behavior. I'm working on this song and the only thing that helps me when I get stuck is listening to other people's music, which is counterintuitive, I know, but what can I say? The creative process is a mystery."

"A song?"

"Yeah, I write music. It's sort of my passion."

"What kind of music?"

"Anything. Everything. I love it all. Hip-hop. Bluegrass. Jazz. I even love the whiny chick singers. Well, some of them."

"How do you feel about country music?"

"Love it."

"Ugh."

"You obviously don't know good country music."

"Oh, I know country music. And it isn't good. How do you feel about a barbershop quartet?"

"I don't know. . . . We don't even have a barbershop in this town." He smiles at me. "So, do you have one?"

"A barbershop?"

"No, silly. A passion."

Nobody's ever asked me that. I run through a list of

answers in the search for something funny. Casually funny. I want to seem as relaxed and sure of myself as he does.

Garden gnomes. *No, that's just stupid.* Strong coffee. *That's a cliché.* Talking-animal movies. *I hate talking-animal movies.*

Then it strikes me.

Of course I have a passion. For as long as I can remember it's been my passion.

"The planet."

"Care to be more specific?"

"Sure. The planet and how we're ruining it and how it may not be livable by the time our children are approaching middle age."

"Are you saying you see children in our future?" He smiles at me again.

"Ha, ha," I say. "Joking is a luxury of living in a sustainable environment. This won't seem so funny years from now. Trust me."

He leans forward on his shovel and I take a good look at him. His skinny arms and big Adam's apple. The sweat at his hairline.

"Yeah." The light goes out of his eyes.

It's one of the hazards of having the planet as my passion. Talking about global warming can be kind of a downer.

He shakes his head and wipes his brow with a bandana from his pocket. "So, where you from?"

Here we go.

"Los Angeles."

"Cool."

"Compared to here, yes, it is."

"Amen." He goes back to raking. I think I'm in the clear until he asks, "Any brothers or sisters?"

You'd think I'd have a canned answer. I've been dreading this question since I boarded my flight to Memphis, but I never bothered to work out what I'd say when it came up.

He eyes me.

"I only ask because I'm living in a tiny trailer with two nine-year-old girls and I've taken to wishing I'd been an only child." He smiles a crooked smile. "But anyway, it's not such a complicated question."

## HOME

On the second Saturday after Dad dropped the bomb, Tess and I went to the same party. We had the same friends. We went to the same parties. That wasn't going to change.

But this time we got dressed in our rooms in our separate homes and drove in our separate cars.

I counted on Tess. I counted on her to tell me what to wear and how to do my hair. She always put on my mascara. I have this weird thing about eyeballs. Even watching somebody else put in contact lenses makes me want to hurl. But Tess had a magical way with the mascara brush. She would talk to me in this gentle voice and tell me something totally stupid and distracting and somehow I'd survive the dangerous proximity of brush to eyeball.

"Voilà!" she'd say. "You look fantastic."

I never saw what the big deal was with mascara. It doesn't seem to change anything. I haven't worn any since Tess moved out.

The night of the party, Gabriel picked me up.

It had been seven days since Gabriel and I had sex and things had been strange between us all week. It was like reliving the period following the hand-to-breast incident of eighth grade, except this time we didn't stop talking to each other. This time we talked to each other as if nothing had happened.

For the last year we'd been fooling around. And that's all it was. *Fooling around.* We made out every now and then. So what? Couldn't friends fool around without it turning into a big deal?

Tess asked me all the time what was happening with Gabriel.

"Nothing," I'd say.

"I don't believe you."

"It's casual. Whatever."

"Is that all you want from him? Something casual?"

"I don't know. We don't really talk about it."

But now we'd had sex. Didn't that scream *It's time to talk?*

Gabriel rang the doorbell. He never did that. He never asked if he could have something from the fridge or if he could use the phone. He'd kick off his shoes and leave them in the middle of the room and he'd help himself to music from Dad's vast collection of female soul singers.

Tonight things were different. Gabriel was ringing the doorbell and I was nervous.

"Gabriel, my man!" I heard Dad say. Their hands slapped in a high five. Why did Dad insist on turning all supermacho around Gabriel?

I wondered what would happen if Dad knew. How differently he might greet Gabriel at the door.

"Arthur," Gabriel said as I was entering the room. "Might I say, you are looking quite well this evening. Quite well, all things considered."

Nobody but Gabriel calls Dad Arthur. To the rest of the world he's just Art. But early on, Gabriel adopted this phony formality with Dad that stuck.

"All things considered" was as close as Gabriel was going to get to telling Dad he knew what was happening with Jane and that he was sorry.

Dad's macho grin slipped away, and he grabbed Gabriel in a big bear hug. I was fragile those days, to say the least, and the sight of this embrace almost undid me.

We took my car because Gabriel's barely holds together with duct tape. He smelled like shaving cream. He'd missed a spot just above his upper lip.

I thought maybe in the car, in the green glow of the dashboard lights, that he might bring up whatever this was that was happening with us. We might finally talk.

We talked about Dad and Jane.

"How're you holding up?"

*I'm not. I'm falling apart.* "Fine."

"Really?"

• 62 •

"What?"

"You look like a mess."

"Thanks. Just what I needed to hear."

"You know what I mean. I don't mean how you *look*, I guess what I mean is how you *seem*. You *seem* like a mess. You *look* hot. The guys are going to be all over you tonight." He gave my knee a pat. A friendly pat.

It deserved a snappy comeback, keep it light, but I was silent.

Last weekend he'd come over because I'd called him in tears. I didn't usually lean on Gabriel that way, but I didn't know who to call. Tess was gone. I never even saw her leaving. Jane packed her things while we were both at school. Dad said they'd be back in a few days to collect the rest.

"It's best if everyone just takes a breather," he'd said.

Gabriel came right away and found me in my room. Dad let him in and then went out for a drink. He never minded leaving me alone in the house with Gabriel.

I was lying on my bed, face splotchy, eyes sore. I'd never cried in front of Gabriel.

He rubbed my back, mumbling something about how life really sucks.

I lifted up my T-shirt so that he could rub my bare back, so that I could feel his touch.

It felt really nice.

Really, really nice.

I unhooked my bra so that he could rub my back without

anything getting in the way. Soon I wasn't thinking about Dad and Jane and Tess. All I was thinking about was Gabriel's hands on my skin.

I turned over.

Gabriel looked surprised. The lights were on. The lights were never on. I could see his face. I lifted my shirt over my head.

He continued to touch me.

I started to unbutton his pants. And then, since everything was different, since everything had changed, I did something I never did with Gabriel. I talked to him, about us, right there in the light.

"I want to," I said. "I want to do it tonight."

○ ○ ○

The party was huge. We had to park five blocks away and even from there we could hear voices. I had an impulse to take Gabriel's hand. He'd rung the doorbell. He'd picked me up to go to a party. This night had all the elements of a date. But I couldn't do it.

There was a crowd swarming the front lawn and jamming up the entryway and I could see people through the second-story windows. I went around to the backyard and bumped into Tess.

All these people. Hundreds of them, and Tess and I find each other right away. Perfect.

"Hi," I said.

"Hey."

I was hoping she'd be wearing something new again. That was a good icebreaker. But she was wearing a striped dress she'd had for over a year and old black boots.

"What's up?" I asked. *What's up?* How lame is that?

I tried to read her face. It was a closed book.

"I can't really handle this tonight. I just want to have a good time. I need to have a good time. You understand." She aimed for a smile but missed. She walked away.

I looked around for Gabriel. He had disappeared somewhere into the crowd. Our date had ended. I looked around for anyone. Somebody who knew me.

I was alone.

# HERE

On Tuesday morning I take my coffee outside. I'm drinking it out of a travel mug I bought at the convenience store; I can't bear to use one more foam cup.

I find Linus sitting cross-legged on the cement by the pool with his eyes closed, his palms raised out and up, much the same way he was on the first day we arrived. I tiptoe over to a lounge chair, ease myself into it and spill hot coffee on my bare legs.

I shout out something totally foul.

Linus stands up and hurries over.

"Everything okay here?"

"Yeah. Ouch. Sorry. I just spilled my coffee."

He grabs a towel and soaks it in the pool, then hands it to me. I put it on my legs. Relief.

"In my experience," Linus says, "the coffee here is barely lukewarm."

"Today the gods conspired to make it scalding hot."

"Let's take a look."

I pull back the towel. I'm pink.

"I think you're going to be okay." Linus smiles and drags a lounge chair next to mine. "So tell me, Harper Evans from Los Angeles, California, how's everything going for you so far?"

"Pretty good. I kind of like it here."

"Good to know. What do you like about it?"

I have to think. I don't really want to say anything about coming to the middle of nowhere where nobody knows me or knows anything about what my life used to be.

"I like the crickets. Or the cicadas, or whatever they are. I like the sounds all around. The buzzing. It feels like the earth is alive here. It's kind of easy to forget that in Los Angeles."

He smiles, leans back in his chair and closes his eyes to the sun.

I remember how I felt when I cut the wood. "And I like the worm-drive saw."

"There's a reason they call them power tools."

Now I lean back in my chair.

I sneak a look at him and I notice that he has a tattoo.

# glad

Large cursive letters on his right arm, just above his farmer's tan.

It suits him. He seems happy, or glad, pretty much all the time. Or maybe *serene* is the better word. Why didn't he think to tattoo *serene* on his arm?

I think about asking him why he chose *glad*, but I decide against it. Like I said, I can be annoying about language. I ask him instead about this ritual with the closed eyes, folded legs and outstretched arms.

"Oh, it's just something I try to do every day. Find a quiet moment and say this thing. It's sort of like a prayer, I guess. A mantra."

"So I interrupted your morning mantra all for a lousy cup of coffee?"

"A lousy cup of *hot* coffee. Hey. It's been my pleasure. Every day is filled with opportunities to take a quiet moment and I'll just grab another one later."

It's time to go out to the bus.

As we're walking away from the pool, me creeping because my legs still sting, Linus asks, "How's it going with Teddy? I know you were reluctant to work with him, but I had a feeling you'd do well together."

"He's fine," I say, and then I feel my cheeks turn pink. They match my legs. My answer is a double entendre.

To Tess, guys are never "cute" or "hot" or "sexy." They're "fine," as in "Ashton Kutcher may have the IQ of a banana slug, but he's *fine*."

I smile even though Linus couldn't know why what I've just said is kind of funny. Only Tess would understand.

○ ○ ○

I worked with Teddy all day. We sat together during lunch. I forgot my hat, so I walked back to his trailer with him in the afternoon and waited outside while he got me an extra one.

None of this is lost on Captain.

At dinner he starts questioning me, and Frances and Marisol join in.

"We saw you," says Captain, and he gives me this knowing look.

"What are you talking about?"

"We saw you and Teddy picnicking together and then taking off for parts unknown," says Frances. She's leaning into Captain and I think about how I haven't said one word about whatever is going on between the two of them in front of her because I don't want to embarrass either one of them.

"Parts unknown? It was his trailer, Frances. I needed a hat. My nose was getting burned. See?" I lean forward, led by my nose.

"Don't come knockin' if this trailer's a-rockin'," Captain chants while he shakes our table.

"Classy, Captain. Really classy."

"C'mon, Harper. Spill. What's up with you and Quiet Tennessee Boy?" Marisol asks.

"He's quiet?"

She shrugs. "He seems pretty quiet to me."

"That's just 'cause you're a big loudmouth," says Captain. Marisol bunches up her napkin and throws it at him.

"He's not quiet," I say. "He's just, I don't know, thoughtful."

Captain bursts out laughing. "And you expect us to believe that you don't have the hots for him?"

Okay, so maybe I was looking at Teddy today, at his eyes that are such a light brown they're almost gold, and maybe I was thinking how much nicer gold eyes are than green-flecked eyes. Maybe I was thinking that he's not too skinny, that his baggy shorts look cute, that his shoulders are nice and broad. Maybe I was listening to his slow, deep drawl and forgetting what to do with the tool in my hands. Maybe I think Teddy is *fine*.

But so what?

Guys don't go for me. Period. I don't distract them. They don't sneak glances in my direction. They don't think of me when I'm not standing right in front of them.

I'm scenery.

I'm background.

What happened with Gabriel only happened because it was easy. It started by accident. A hand falling off the edge of the couch and brushing up against me.

I'm convenient. I'm there. The night in my bedroom when I cried, and turned to face him in the light, and reached for the buttons of his jeans was followed by several more nights when we were near each other with nothing else to do. No place else worth being. Maybe Dad was out. Or Gabriel's parents were away. We had sex and then it was over. Sometimes it seemed I could have been anyone.

And Gabriel has been it. That's all. Even the guy who made Gabriel start fooling around with me again never really existed. Okay, so his name is Will Portnoy, but the part about him having an interest in me was made up.

Will asked me if I wanted to come over to his house to watch *Braveheart,* for a project we were doing for world history. Anyway, when I told Gabriel about it I chose to leave out the history project, in a sad attempt to make him jealous that miraculously seemed to work.

The next weekend Gabriel and Tess and this guy Tess liked named Brady and I hung out at Brady's house, and when she was outside with Brady talking by the pool and Gabriel and I were inside watching yet *another* DVD he pulled *another* hand-slippage stunt that went farther, faster, and with that Gabriel claimed me again.

For this I have to thank Will Portnoy.

Long digression, I know.

Anyway, guys don't tend to go for me.

Not that I care. I'm here to build a house. That happens to be for Teddy. I'm not here to date him, I'm here to house him.

I try out this last line on the group.

"Whatever you have to tell yourself to get you through the night," says Captain.

"So what about you two?" Fight back. Put up a mirror. "What's going on there?"

If I thought this was going to embarrass Captain, forget it. He looks at me like, *Thanks for the assist!*

"It's simple," he says. "I'm crazy about Frances and she's crazy about me, she just hasn't quite admitted it to herself yet. For a few more days we'll play this cat-and-mouse game and then finally I'll lean in for a kiss and she'll meet me halfway and we'll spend the rest of the summer blissfully in love."

Frances hides her face in her hands, laughing.

This is just a more romantic version of what Captain has told me privately over the past few days, but I can't believe he just said this out loud in front of Frances, not to mention Marisol.

*So this is how a real relationship begins*, I think.

## HOME

I have no memories of Dad with Mom, only memories of Dad and Jane.

The time Dad rang his own doorbell on their anniversary, his face hidden behind an enormous bouquet of lilies.

Drinking too much on a New Year's Eve. Dad changing out of his sweatpants into a tux and twirling Jane around the room to an old Nina Simone record.

The trip they took without us to Cabo San Lucas and how they came home with colorful shirts, peeled noses and straw hats.

The way he called her darlin'.

It was a marriage, like any other marriage, and it seemed real and solid and indestructible.

It was just there, and it would always be there.

I asked Dad. I asked him in the kitchen with the melting ice cubes in his Scotch glass and the root beer pooling on the floor. The kitchen was the center of our family life.

"What happened?"

Dad's eyes filled with tears and he pressed his hands into his closed lids, hard.

"I don't really know what to say." He wiped his face on his sleeve. He picked up his glass and shook the ice cubes around and then drank the last drops. "It's complicated, relationships are complicated. Life is long, and sometimes marriages feel even longer, and people get lazy, and worse, they get indifferent, and sometimes you start to think maybe you've lost some part of yourself, that you don't even remember who you are and what it felt like to be somebody not married to this person, and then some days you love this very same person more than you are able to explain. You'll be driving in your car at dusk and a wave of warmth will envelop you just because this person exists in the world, but the next day that warmth will vanish again, and the last thing I want to do is say too much, which I'm afraid, at this point, I've already done."

I looked at my father. I was too young to remember what he looked like while he was coping with what happened to Mom, but it was hard for me to imagine him looking any worse than he did sitting at the counter with snot on his sleeve.

I thought of him in his tuxedo. Behind the lilies. His straw hat and peeling nose.

I thought about memory.

Do we choose our memories? Did I choose these memories of Dad and Jane? Did my mind reject . . . what? Silences? Disagreements? Departures from the house without a kiss? Late nights stuck at work?

I didn't remember those moments. To a kid, how could a silence or a glare or a harsh whisper compete with Dad hiding behind an enormous bouquet of lilies?

It's not like Dad and Jane were throwing things or hitting each other or disappearing for days on end.

I never even thought about them as people in a relationship; I thought of them as Dad and Jane, just Dad and Jane, and this other world Dad was describing now, hunched over his empty glass, was a secret world to which I had no access and wanted none.

A week later I went to lunch with Jane. Since she left, we'd spoken only to arrange this date. It was implied that this was to be our time for a big talk.

I didn't want to go. I didn't know what to say or how to act. But Dad told me I shouldn't shut out Jane, that I'd feel better if I spent some time with her, and, well, this is kind of Dad's whole thing. He's a psychiatrist. Unlike most kids, I listen when my dad tells me he thinks something will make me feel better, because he's usually right.

I got there first, this little restaurant on Montana Avenue

that we would go to sometimes for a "girls' lunch" that always included Tess and Rose.

I switched my seat. I rearranged my silverware. I folded and unfolded my napkin.

But the minute Jane walked in and started toward my table, whatever awkwardness I felt melted away. She was no longer the mysterious other half of the secret difficult relationship I had no access to. She was the woman who made me the paper crown on that June Gloom day, and I thought of all the days in between then and now when she was the only mother I ever knew.

By the time she reached me, without thinking I opened my arms. She held me for a long time. She stroked my hair. She leaned back and looked into my face and said, "Are we getting the usual?"

That meant the Southwestern chopped salad with grilled chicken.

"Of course."

We sat down. She held on to my hand for another beat, then let it go. She put the menu aside and stared intently at me.

"Is that a new coat?"

"Yeah. On sale. Forty-nine bucks. You like?"

"I love."

I smiled.

"I miss you, kid."

I felt the tickle in my nose that signals tears. I reached for my water and took a long drink.

"It's a tough time," she said. "For me. For you. For all of us. I'm here if you want to talk about it."

"I don't understand."

"I mean we can talk. Like friends. Like family. However. Whatever you need."

"No, I mean I don't understand what happened."

She leaned back in her chair. Her dark hair was gray at her part and had been for a while now. She took off her glasses, which were black and came up to a point at the sides. The points were decorated with a few small sparkling rhinestones. I never understood when Jane needed her glasses and when she didn't, but I hadn't thought to ask her, and now I probably never would.

"What did your father tell you? No, wait. You don't have to answer that. What you discuss with your father is between the two of you. I don't want to overstep any boundaries."

The only way I could see to fill the silence that followed was to answer her question.

"He gave me some long, convoluted lecture about how marriage is hard."

"Well, I guess that about sums things up."

"Now what?"

She reached again for my hand. "I don't know, sweetheart. I wish I did."

I opened my mouth to ask her how Tess was doing but I choked. I could only manage to half-croak.

"Tess?"

"She's angry. She's hurt. She's disappointed and upset.

She's going through a really rough time, but she'll pull through it. She'll come back around. I know she will."

What did that mean? *She'll come back around.* To me? I wanted to ask Jane more, but I couldn't. I guess on some level I knew. Tess had left me, and now, among all the other things I had to cope with, I had to wait for Tess to come back around.

We sat in silence as the waiter delivered our salads.

"Harper," Jane said. "Whenever you want it, whenever you need it, you'll always have a home with me too."

That was a lie, even though she didn't mean it to be. I didn't have a home with Jane. When everything else fell away, when all the ties were untied and everything was undone, my only home in the world was with Dad. But I knew what she was trying to say, and I thanked her.

# STEP THREE:
## PUT UP WALLS

The foundation is done. We put in plastic piping to ventilate the crawl space, the concrete contractors filled in the cement blocks, we spaced out and installed the joists and then put down the floor sheathing, and now there's a big, solid concrete block with a flat wood top where nothing but weeds once stood.

I've done things in my life, some of them pretty well. I won the spelling bee in sixth grade. I helped my school implement a comprehensive recycling program. I taught my baby brother how to ride a bike. With Tess I made a huge Thanksgiving meal. But I've never done anything as impressive as building this forty-by-sixty-foot rectangular concrete block with a flat wood top.

It's starting to look like something is really happening. We've got this foundation, and there's the pile of debris from the original house. It was a mountain when we first started, but it's been getting smaller and smaller every day, like a pile of jelly beans in a heart-shaped box, as the pieces of the Wright family's former life get hauled away.

Now we're starting on the walls.

We're framing them with long plywood boards, exterior walls that will close off the house from the outside world, and interior walls to make the private spaces every house needs.

Captain comes by. "Whatcha doing?"

His job's been easy. He's spent the morning on top of the foundation, marking wall lines with chalk.

I'm working on the interior walls that will intersect other walls. They're called butt walls.

Captain knows this.

"Working," I answer. "What's it look like?"

"But *what* are you working on?"

"A wall."

"What *kind* of wall?"

I roll my eyes at him. "You are such a juvenile."

Teddy steps in front of me, mock-protectively.

"She's building a butt wall. Gotta problem with it?"

Captain puts up his hands. "No, boss. No problem at all."

He sits down. Frances and Marisol wander over, with Seth trailing behind them. Ever since it became clear that Frances and Captain are teetering on the edge of coupledom, and ever since Marika let Seth rub in her sunblock and then never spoke another word to him, Seth has been circling Marisol.

It's noon. We break for lunch at twelve-thirty. This is when the heat hits its peak and it becomes almost impossible to work.

"I'm fomenting a coup," says Frances. "And when I'm the almighty, powerful leader, there'll be no work between eleven and two."

"Did you just use the word *fomenting?*" asks Captain.

"Yes, I believe I did."

"*Fomenting?*"

"It's a word educated people use."

Teddy chimes in. "It's one of those words that seems to exist only in relationship to another word. Like, you only ever hear *fomenting* with the word *coup.*" He lifts his T-shirt to his face and wipes the sweat from it. "Like how you only hear *profusely* when you're talking about sweating."

This strikes me as unbelievably kind. He's bailing Captain out. Trying to keep him from looking stupid in front of Frances.

But Captain's unfazed. He's used to Frances's sarcasm.

Marisol removes her baseball hat and sighs. "I miss San Francisco. In the summer a fog settles in and it gets so cold you have to wear a fleece jacket."

"I miss Salt Lake City," says Seth, whose round face is an unhealthy shade of purple. "The actual Salt Lake our city is named for smells like sulfur and is filled with gnats, but right about now I'd jump in headfirst."

"If it's just a little cool-off y'all are after, I can make that happen," Teddy says. "There's a pond about a ten-minute walk from here."

"We're on the clock until twelve-thirty," I point out.

Captain jumps up. "So what, Girl Scout? Desperate times call for desperate measures. And this heat is des-per-ate."

"Let's go," says Frances.

"Lead the way," says Marisol.

Teddy turns to me. "I can't do this without my double-y partner. You in, Harper?"

I take off my goggles. It's a small miracle nobody mocked me. I've been wearing them for the entire conversation. "Oh, all right."

The pond is almost too warm, but it still feels great. Frances and Marisol and I formed a huddle and determined that we were all wearing less-than-revealing sports bras. So we took off our T-shirts to a loud chorus of whistles from Seth, Captain and Teddy. They've removed their shirts too, even Seth, who looks fine. Not *fine*, but he looks okay without his shirt on. I'd tell him that if I wasn't certain it would mortify him.

Frances suggested that the guys strip to their boxers, but Seth looked like he'd rather kill himself, Captain said he was going commando and Teddy confessed to wearing briefs.

"Briefs, dude?" Captain asked.

"Sometimes a man needs a little extra support."

So we all jumped in wearing our shorts.

After swimming around for about half an hour, I get out to dry off, and for the first time since I've been here, the midday sun feels good. Teddy gets out of the pond too and sits next to me on the grass.

"That was nice," I say.

"Yeah, it was."

"It's so beautiful here."

"You think so?"

"I do."

"I guess I used to think so too."

One of our typical silences settles in. Teddy reaches for his T-shirt and pulls it over his head.

"The last time I came swimming here was last summer. I took my sisters and their best friend, this funny-looking girl named Belinda with red hair. Alice and Grace used to love sleeping over at her house. They said her dad made the best pancakes. They couldn't get over the idea of a dad cooking. Our dad can't make toast." He stops and squeezes some of the excess water from his shorts. He looks out toward the pond. "Now they're both gone. Belinda and her dad who made great pancakes."

Nine people died in April. Bailey has a population of just under one thousand. I guess if I'd stopped to do the math I could have figured that Teddy would know some of the people who didn't survive.

"My sisters couldn't sleep for two months. Part of that's from the moving around. We spent the first few nights with some friends. Their house sat about twenty feet outside the path and it was totally untouched. Not even a crooked picture on the wall. Then we moved to another friend's. Even after we got the trailer and got all settled in, still they couldn't sleep."

"So how'd they start sleeping again?"

"I build them an invisible wall. When they're both in their beds and they turn out the lights, I go in and put up a wall around them that keeps out bad dreams, monsters, tornadoes, everything."

"What's it made of?"

He looks at me and smiles.

"Invisible bricks."

We watch as Captain climbs out onto a branch of a tree and swings with both arms. It looks dangerous, but he lets go and lands with a splash and comes up laughing.

"What's it like?" I ask.

"You mean a tornado?"

"Yeah."

"Like nothing you've ever experienced. I mean, I know you have earthquakes out where you're from, and I'm sure being in an earthquake is no party, and maybe a tornado is no worse, but it's certainly different. It sounds like a locomotive. It smells like hell. And when you're in the middle of one, it feels like the fingers of a giant hand have reached under your home to rip it right off the foundation."

"That sounds terrifying."

"It is. And what it leaves behind is impossible to describe. Remember, we've been cleaning up already three months now, pretty much full-time, since before y'all got here."

Everyone is out of the water now, and they've all picked a spot of grass a safe distance away from where Teddy and I are sitting. I look over at them just in time to catch Captain exaggeratedly moving his eyebrows up and down and puckering his lips.

Suddenly it all seems too stupid, his taunts about Teddy and me. There isn't room for that kind of thing when your world is falling apart. You may think there is, and think it's what you need, and that may send you running off to your oldest friend, and it may make you turn your naked body to his, but you'd be making a big mistake.

When something comes along and rips your home right off its foundation, you have to use everything you have just to try to hold yourself together.

## HOME

Tess came up to me at school on the Monday after the party and apologized.

*Maybe this is it*, I thought. *Maybe this is Tess coming back around.*

"I shouldn't have left you like that. And I definitely shouldn't have left you and then gone off and done four Jell-O shots." She made a face. "Jell-O is disgusting. I don't even understand what it is. I mean, what are its properties? Is it a solid? A liquid? By the way, adding vodka into the mix sheds absolutely no light on these complex questions."

For the briefest moment, I forgot everything and just laughed at her like I used to.

"So, how was your night? I'm guessing it was better than mine because I didn't see you anywhere near the Jell-O shots."

I had seen Gabriel talking to Sarah Denton with his face about three inches from hers, and I took off without saying goodbye to him, figuring he could find his own way home.

I didn't say any of this to Tess because I couldn't even figure out what it was I was feeling. And anyway, with her gone only about ten days, there was too much to fill her in on standing in the hallway between classes.

"It was okay," I lied.

There was an awkward silence. I suddenly felt like a shy boy trying to muster up the courage to ask an untouchable girl out on a date. I didn't know how to begin. Was the cooling-off period over? Could we start talking again?

Tess and I never had to part not knowing when and where we would see each other again. We always knew we'd meet up back home, in the kitchen.

"So, maybe we could hang out later," I said.

"For sure. You know, you should come by our new place. Check it out. Cole has a terrarium with a tarantula in his room. Mom's overcompensating. You know how freaked out she is by spiders, so she must really be worried about him."

"That'd be nice," I said. "And you can always come by the house too. You know how to find it."

Her face fell. She was suddenly Tess from the party again.

"I can't do that. I won't do that. If you want to hang out it has to be at my place, or somewhere else, anywhere but your house."

It was as if she'd slapped me. Kicked me in the gut. Yet she hadn't moved.

Tess was still far, far away from me.

"But . . ." But I didn't know what to say. I didn't understand.

"I don't want to go to that house ever again."

In a second, a whole world was revealed.

Tess blamed Dad.

I let this wash over me. I soaked in it as the bell for fourth period rang and Tess disappeared down the hallway.

I was never late. To anything. Ever. But today I was going to be late.

No, today I was going to miss class altogether.

I leaned against my locker and slid down.

I started to get angry. I started to think of things in terms I'd never had to think of them before.

My father. *Her* mother.

Is that what this was going to come down to?

You didn't see me refusing to go to Jane's. In fact, I'd gone to lunch with Jane, and I let her hold my hand and tell me she still loved me.

I was trying to be generous. I was trying to stay above all that, the *mine* and the *hers*.

But not Tess.

I sat on the cold stone floor of the empty hallway.

# HERE

This morning the heat came early.

By ten, my hair was soaked through. I lifted up my goggles to wipe away the sweat that had pooled just below them, and like an idiot, or maybe like someone in the throes of heat-stroke, I forgot to put them back on before returning to the worm-drive saw.

I got some dust in my eye. At least, that's what I assumed it was, but now it's after lunch and my eye is still stinging and tearing and nothing seems to make it stop.

I can't check if it looks okay because one of the many drawbacks to portable toilets is that they don't come equipped with mirrors.

I need to have someone look at my eye.

Stacey is my partner this week, but she's nowhere to be seen. Probably snuck off to the woods to be alone with Jared.

I go find Teddy. He's hammering with total concentration and precision. He works like his life depends on it, and in a way, it sort of does.

"Can you look at something for me?" I ask.

"Sure." He wipes his hands on his shorts and I take a step closer to him.

"It's my eye."

"What about it?"

"It won't stop tearing."

"Maybe you're just overly emotional. Or maybe you're hormonal? I hear chicks get that way sometimes."

"Seriously, does it look okay?"

He takes my face in both hands and looks closely.

"It does look red. And kind of sad. What happened?"

"I forgot my goggles."

"You? Impossible!"

"I think there's something stuck in there."

He pulls down my lower lid and then lifts my upper one, exposing the red ugly part around my eye. He's dangerously close to my eyeball, but somehow it doesn't freak me out.

"I don't see anything, but I think you should have it looked at. C'mon. Let's go see my mom."

We find Linus and tell him that Teddy is going to take me into town to see his mom about my eye. When Linus looks puzzled, Teddy says, "She can't stop crying."

I glare at him.

"It's okay, Harper," Teddy says. "Crying is nothing to be ashamed of. We all need a good cry every now and then."

"It's probably her cornea," says Linus. "Some debris may have gotten in there and scratched it. You'll drive her to the clinic?"

"Yes, sir," says Teddy. If Captain called Linus sir, you'd know he was being obnoxious, but with Teddy it's charmingly authentic.

"Go ahead." Linus waves us off.

I'm having a little trouble navigating the rocky path and Teddy takes me by the arm.

"That's so cool your mom's a nurse," I tell him. "My dad's a doctor, but he'd be completely useless in a situation like this. He's a shrink."

"So you must be either totally evolved or seriously messed up."

"Both," I say.

We get into a blue pickup truck with a smashed-in hood.

I gesture at it. "Should I be worried about your driving?"

"No, that's tornado damage. It's a miracle this baby survived at all. The same can't be said for the cow that landed on it."

"Ouch."

"Actually, it was a tree."

"So why'd you say it was a cow?"

"In my head it sounded funny, but not so much when I said it out loud."

"No, sick is more like it."

"At least I'm not the one who can't stop crying."

I turn the radio to my favorite station. I've been listening to it obsessively. It plays only Christian rock, a genre with which I have no previous experience, and I'm amazed at how many songs can be written about Jesus.

They say that Eskimos have fifty words for snow, so I guess Christian rockers have infinite ways of saying they love Jesus.

I explain my obsession to Teddy so he doesn't think I actually like this music, but soon we're belting out the chorus to this really rocking song that just repeats the lines: *What's up? Only Jesus, baby.*

We pull up to a little storefront with the words BAILY MED. CLINIC in gold stickers on the door. If you didn't look too closely, this small stretch of Main Street would appear to be postcard perfect. Colorfully painted buildings. A brick sidewalk. Brand-new American flags, still showing their creases, flying from the lampposts.

But then you see that the businesses on either side of this clinic are boarded up, and the sidewalk has a few huge cracks in it that look like earthquake fault lines in California, and there are empty metal frames where awnings used to be.

We sit in the truck for a minute as Teddy does his best to describe how this town used to look.

"It was untouched by time. On the surface. The crazy thing is that underneath, well, this place has changed. When my parents first moved here twenty-five years ago, it was unheard of, a mixed-race couple. This was a mostly white town with a few black residents. Now we even have a black chief of police. But on the outside everything still looked exactly the same until this tornado came along."

Teddy walks around to my side of the truck and opens the door for me.

"This is temporary," he says, motioning to the clinic. "The real one was up the road, but it was destroyed. We're hoping to rebuild it sometime this year, but who knows."

There's a woman in her sixties sitting at a reception desk with purple-framed glasses.

"Afternoon, Mrs. Coyle," Teddy says.

"How you doin', sweetness? You stayin' out of trouble?"

"Yes, ma'am."

"And who's this pretty little thing with you?"

I feel my face go red.

"This is my friend Harper." Teddy gestures at me. "She can't stop crying."

I wait for her to pick up on the joke.

Nothing.

She's still smiling at Teddy.

She grabs her phone, presses a few buttons, slams it down and tries the whole routine again, gives up, swivels in her chair and shouts, "Diane! Your boy's here!"

"Go on back," she tells us.

Teddy's mom gives him a hug and musses his hair and Teddy introduces me.

"Mom, this is Harper. You met her at the picnic, remember?"

"Of course I do." She smiles and takes my outstretched hand in both of hers. "Teddy speaks highly of you. Thank you for everything you've been doing for us."

She looks at my eye and confirms Linus's diagnosis of a scratched cornea. She gives me some eyedrops and a patch to wear for the next several days.

"Do I have to?" I ask.

"If you want your eye to get better."

As we step back out into the heat, Teddy says, "C'mon. You heard what my old lady said."

"Yeah, she said you speak highly of me."

"That's not what I'm talking about. The patch. Put it on."

I take it out of its package, stretch the elastic around the back of my head and lower the patch over my eye. "Are you going to make fun of me?"

He throws his arm around my shoulder and leads me back to the truck. "You can count on it."

○ ○ ○

I spend the next two days back at the motel while everyone else is off at the site.

Nurse's orders.

Sure, I appreciate the extra sleep. I appreciate the time alone in the room. It's what I've been craving since I got here. But I have to admit, I get kind of lonely.

And maybe it's the control freak in me, but I wonder what's happening to the house while I'm away. Will the site look different? I want to be there when they raise the walls.

The good news is that my tan is in tip-top shape.

I'm sitting out by the pool listening to my favorite Christian rock station, which I've dubbed WWJD.

I'm singing along:

*"I've seen your face,*
*I've heard your voice,*
*I'll walk your path till my feet are sore."*

It occurs to me that in singing these words, and singing them out loud, I'm probably as close right now as I'll ever get to praying.

It's not like I'm against religion. I'm just not a believer. And that's not for lack of exposure. Growing up we'd have Shabbat dinners from time to time with candles and wine and challah, and when I'd bristle at the idea, Jane would tell me to think of it as just another of our theme dinners.

"This time," she'd say, "the theme is Judaism!"

I've been in houses of worship. Tess and Rose were both bat mitzvahed in a synagogue. I went to a wedding at a church where I almost took communion until Dad yanked me out of line.

I stop singing, but then I start up again because I realize this isn't praying. It's just singing along to the radio. It's no different than reciting the Pledge of Allegiance.

*One nation under God.*
*I'll walk your path.*

They're just words. And words alone don't really mean anything. It's what you feel and what you believe when you say them that matters.

The gate to the pool swings open and I look up expecting to see another family with small children that has made the mistake of stopping in what I'm sure they thought would be a quiet motel on their trip cross-country, but instead I see Teddy.

I'm happy to see him because, well, he's Teddy. But also I

was just starting to think that wedding vows are the perfect example of words that don't mean anything unless you believe what you're saying, and that got me thinking of Dad and Jane, and I just want to enjoy the sun.

He's walking toward me with something in his outstretched hands.

A pie.

"My mother made it for you," he says. "It's peach. And it totally kicks ass."

I'm so caught off guard that I don't even try to grab a towel or anything to cover up.

I'm wearing a bikini, but I feel naked. Teddy has seen me in my sports bra and shorts, but this is different. If I grab a towel and wrap it around myself, I'll be letting on that I don't want Teddy to see my body, which would be worse than just letting him see it. I give up. "My very own pie?"

"There's no stopping Mom when she gets it in her head to bake someone a pie. Now, let's see that eye, Bluebeard."

I lift the patch.

He leans in close. "Looking good." He pulls a chair over and starts to remove his boots and socks. "Okay if I join you?"

"They won't miss you at the site?"

"Linus told me I should check on you and not to bother coming back. Not like he was firing me or anything, he just thought you could use the company."

*Good old Linus.*

Teddy takes off his shirt. I hand him my bottle of water and he takes a long drink.

We sit side by side in the scorching-hot sun.

"How old are you anyway?" I ask.

"I'm eighteen. But you probably thought I was older, right? I mean, one look at these bad boys and you gotta figure I've been lifting weights for at least a decade." He flexes both of his skinny arms.

I laugh. "I guessed you were out of high school."

"Graduated in June."

"The school wasn't damaged?"

"The roof was torn off the gym. God's way of telling the jocks that they'd better remember who's really in charge."

"So you're not a jock?"

"Does that surprise you?"

"I guess not."

"Would it surprise you if I told you my dad is the football coach?"

"Not really. The burly guys hanging around the site in the Bailey High Football T-shirts are kind of a giveaway. But I thought he taught English."

"He does both. So it all evens out. I'm lousy at sports, but I'm pretty good with the learnin'." He taps his temple. "And teaching summer school provides a nice professional symmetry: Most of the students who couldn't keep up during the school year also happen to be Dad's football players."

He's lying on his side with his elbow propping up his head. I can see each one of his ribs.

"You sound kind of bitter," I say.

"About the fact that Dad's a football star and I'm a ninety-pound weakling? Nah."

"Hmmm."

"Look. He likes sports; I like music. So what?" Teddy shrugs. "He's a great coach. Everyone loves him. Even the redneck jocks who might not have liked the idea of taking orders on the field from a black man eventually come around to worshipping Dad. They'll spend every free minute they have fixing up our house. Some of those same guys will call me a pussy any chance they get, but at least they respect my dad."

"High school really can be as bad as they say."

"As bad as who says?"

"I don't know, the movies. Horror novels."

"I have a theory that as long as you have one good friend, one *real* friend, you can get through anything."

"So who's yours?"

"Mikey. He's away for the summer."

"Some friend."

I reach for my radio and flip it off. Suddenly Jesus radio is unbearably annoying. Maybe it's this one song. I've heard it too many times.

Without the radio there's quiet. No saws. No hammering. No voices. Not even cicadas.

"What's it like to graduate?" I ask.

"Graduation was one of the best days of my life. We had the ceremony in the roofless gym, sort of a symbolic gesture, I guess, our way of saying nothing was going to stop that day from coming, and coming the way it always has. Without the roof, the sun lit up every corner of the room, and my dad took the stage to hand me my diploma, and I cried like a baby through the whole entire thing."

I could take this moment and turn it around and tease him about crying, like he teased me about my eye, but nothing feels funny about what Teddy just told me.

So instead I tell him how my parents are going through a divorce. I actually say the word *divorce*, which comes surprisingly easy, but I don't go into any details of how Jane isn't really my mother and Tess isn't really my sister, and I don't tell him how far away from me all the people are who I love.

We sit there a minute; then he says, "Want to take a swim?"

I stand up and pull off my patch. He takes my hand, and we jump into the water together.

# HOME

Jane and Tess moved into a house in Laurel Canyon. With its walls of glass and slate floors and high ceilings and white paint, it was in every way different from what used to be our house, with its wood trim and creaky stairs.

I went for the first time several weeks after Tess said she'd never come over again. I was angry. If she wouldn't come to my house, I decided, then I wouldn't go to hers.

Then Dad intervened.

We were sitting in the park drinking vanilla ice-blendeds.

Cole was spinning himself sick on the tire swing. Pavlov was sitting obediently at Dad's feet.

Ever since the separation Pavlov had become extra-vigilant. This was one of the by-products of his shuttling back and forth along with Cole. He wouldn't let Dad out of his sight. I'm sure he was the same way with Jane.

Pavlov had also become a middle-of-the-night pacer. He wandered the halls and his nails clicked on the wooden floors, reminding us that things had changed so much that even the dog couldn't sleep at night.

"I think he's going to puke," I said to Dad. Cole had just eaten a red, white and blue Popsicle, and he was spinning so fast all I could see was a tangle of hair.

"He's a strong boy. Iron constitution, just like his father." Dad patted his stomach. This was a joke. Dad spends more time in the bathroom than the world's vainest teenage girl.

"Listen, Harper."

That's always the beginning of a serious conversation. The command to listen, as if I wouldn't anyway, is Dad's way of signaling that something important is about to follow.

"I want to talk to you about Tess. I'm worried that the two of you are letting everything that's happening with Jane and me get in the way of your relationship."

"That's stupid, Dad. No offense, but really. Of course everything is getting in the way. How could it not?"

Dad sighed. "I know it's hard, but this shouldn't change things between you. You have your own relationship that has nothing to do with anybody else. I know it'll take work to push everything to the side, but it's critical. You need each other."

"I don't know if you'd be saying all this if you knew how she felt about you."

A silence wedged itself between us on the bench.

After a little while, Dad leaned down and scratched Pavlov between the ears.

"Dogs," he said. "Their love is unconditional."

"That's only because you feed them and let them outside to shit."

"You're crude."

"No, Dad, you are. It's crude to compare the love of a dog with what I'm going through with Tess."

"I know what you're going through—believe me, I know. But please, don't worry about what she thinks of me. Let her hate me if she has to. You don't have to defend me. It would mean much more to me if you two worked things out than if you gave her the silent treatment out of some kind of loyalty to me."

"But why is she so mad at you?"

"That's a good question."

He put his hand on my knee and gave it a squeeze.

"Listen." Again with the *listen*. "Let it go. You two don't have to figure this all out. All you have to work on is how to stay who you are to each other."

So the next day after school I went over to Tess's new house.

We sat in Cole's room. He let the tarantula crawl up his

arm and we squealed and told him it was gross and he beamed with pride. Tess painted his toenails blue and I threw two games of Go Fish. When it was time for me to go back home, Cole cried, held onto my leg and told me he wanted me to stay.

# HERE

I've always had this thing about people eating dessert alone. I can't think of anything more depressing than someone sitting all by herself about to dig into a piece of pie. It's almost unspeakably sad.

And a whole pie? That's not sad. That's disgusting.

So I invite Captain and Frances and Marisol to share my pie, after dinner, in my room. And since Teddy brought it, it only seems right to invite him too.

It would be poor manners *not* to invite him.

This has nothing to do with his eyes. Or his smile. Or his accent.

But I don't know how to get in touch with him. I can't look him up in the phone book because his house is gone. He has a cell phone, but I don't have the number.

I'll ask Linus.

He knows everything.

Dinner is in an hour and I find him sitting on a patch of dead grass out behind the motel, meditating. As I get closer I decide maybe I shouldn't interrupt him, but when I turn to leave he calls my name.

"Sorry," I say. "I don't mean to bother you."

"You're not bothering me at all."

I sit down next to him on the grass and consider how different we are. Linus seeks out these times to think, and I seek out anything that might keep me from thinking.

"Do you mind if I ask what it is you say as part of this mantra thing?"

I'm curious how someone like Linus finds God, or solace, or peace, or whatever it is he finds out here alone, in the grass, while he's reciting words. Is it just a matter of believing what you say?

"It's an ancient Sufi text. I think you're technically supposed to recite it in the morning, when the sun comes up." Linus scratches his beard. "Me? Sometimes I'm too busy, and sometimes the moment I need it comes at the end of a day."

"And it makes everything better?"

"No, it just helps me remember certain things it's important for me to remember." He stands up and brushes the grass off his clothes.

"Will you tell me what it is, this ancient Sufi text? I think maybe I could use a mantra."

He smiles. "Another time. I promise. Right now I have to get things ready for dinner. If we don't feed you, you might revolt."

"Or *foment*."

He looks at me curiously and shrugs. "Whatever."

He starts walking away and I watch him, almost forgetting why I came looking for him in the first place. "Wait!"

He turns. "Yes, Ms. Harper?"

"I need to reach Teddy. Do you have a number for him?" I'm embarrassed by Linus's knowing smile, so I quickly add, "It's about a pie."

"Oh, well, in that case." He pulls out his cell phone, punches a few buttons and hands it to me. It's already ringing and Linus is walking away.

"Give it back to me at dinner," he calls over his shoulder.

I'm flustered when Teddy answers, but I manage to piece together a coherent sentence about how eating pie alone is sad, and would he like to share it with me, and some others, in my room at nine o'clock.

"I never say no to Mom's pie."

A few minutes before nine I think to put on some makeup. This is hard to do because everyone is already in my room, so I sneak into the bathroom, and when I emerge Marisol says, "Someone is looking hot. And for once, it's not me."

Captain whistles. Loud. Both fingers in his mouth.

We all shush him. We're breaking the rules. The official policy about boys in girls' rooms is that it isn't supposed to happen unless (A) the door is wide open and (B) you have at least three feet on the floor.

When Linus distributed the handbook I asked him what would happen if you both lay down on the floor. He shrugged. "You'd probably wind up with some serious rug burn."

But even if nobody takes the rules too seriously, I tell Captain to keep it down.

Frances eyes me. "I'm searching for a more graceful way of saying this, but I'm coming up empty-handed. So here goes: Are you wearing *that?*"

I look down at myself. Baggy shorts that go to my knees. Pink camouflage tank top.

"What?"

"I can tell by the last-minute makeup job that you haven't forgotten a certain young stud named Teddy is en route. So . . . the tank top is okay. It's cute and it'll come in particularly handy if we get lost in a pink jungle. But the shorts have to go."

I panic. Frances is right. The shorts are shockingly bad.

"What do I do?" I ask to Frances's back. She's up and out the door and back in a matter of seconds with a pair of her jeans.

"Quick. Put these on."

"They won't fit. They'll look terrible on me."

"Harper. Bathroom. Now. Jeans. Go." Frances shoos me inside. Through the closed door she says, "You know, it wouldn't kill you to wear something a little tight on a night like tonight."

I squeeze myself into her jeans, and miraculously, I'm able to button them up without too much effort, and even more miraculously, they look pretty good on me.

There's a knock on the door.

Teddy.

I rush out of the bathroom, Captain manages a quiet whistle and I whisk Teddy inside and close the door behind him.

He's wearing jeans and a black T-shirt and black Vans exactly like the ones I have at home. He's got a messenger bag over his shoulder and a guitar case in his hand.

"So this is the pie party?" he asks.

"Yes, it is," says Captain. He's lying on Marisol's bed with Frances curled under his arm. They're officially a couple now.

"I come bearing refreshments." Teddy reaches into his messenger bag and pulls out a bottle. "It's a Tennessee tradition. Peach pie and Jack Daniel's."

"Ugh. That is such a guy drink," says Marisol. "Have you ever met a girl who drinks Jack Daniel's?"

"Sorry, Marisol," says Teddy. "If I knew how to make a cosmopolitan, I'd have brought you that."

"Sexist."

"What? You're the one who said girls don't like Jack Daniel's. And anyway, I bet Harper would drink some Jack." He looks at me. "Am I right?"

He pulls out a stack of Dixie cups and pours a little for me into one with Winnie-the-Pooh on it.

He holds it out. "Don't let me down, girl."

I take a whiff. It's strong. I'm more of a wine cooler kind of drinker, but I can't resist a challenge.

I take a sip and it burns.

"Not bad," I manage with my throat and stomach and all sorts of other organs I can't even name on fire.

We all toast and then dig into the pie.

At ten-thirty the "lights-out" knock arrives at our door. Tonight it's Susannah, covering for Linus. She's a college student, here for the summer with her boyfriend, Brad, and it's probably been no more than three years since she was a high school volunteer herself, so I don't think she cares much who's in the room doing what. I'm glad Susannah is on duty tonight. It feels better somehow pulling one over on Susannah than it would feel to be pulling one over on Linus.

"Where's Seth?" asks Teddy.

I guess he's pretty clueless or else he wouldn't be asking this question. Poor Seth. He has it bad for Marisol. He buzzes around her constantly like a big, sweaty fly, and she's too nice to tell him to back off. Also, boyfriending him seems to do absolutely nothing to deter him. Even blatantly shameless boyfriending of this sort:

*I really miss my boyfriend. Or, My boyfriend is going to call tonight. Or, You like the Black Eyed Peas? My boyfriend loves the Black Eyed Peas! Or, You eat with a fork? My boyfriend eats with a fork!*

Nothing works.

So Marisol knows, as do the rest of us, that inviting Seth to sneak into her room late at night would be more than the poor guy could take.

But maybe Teddy has missed all this, maybe he saw tonight as some kind of triple date. Captain and Frances. Seth and Marisol. Him and me.

Or maybe I'm overthinking things.

I take another swig.

By midnight, when we start to hear the doors opening and closing in the nightly pilgrimage to the pool, I'm pretty buzzed. Captain wants to go, but I tell him, "Friends don't let friends swim drunk."

Marisol is in the bathroom with Teddy's cell phone, making a drunken call to Pierre full of whispering and giggling. Frances has fallen asleep, and I'm not far from passing out myself.

I'm lying on my bed and Teddy is sitting on the floor picking absentmindedly at the strings of his guitar.

"Play me something," I say.

"One of your favorite Jesus songs?"

"Anything." I adjust my flimsy pillow.

He plays a few chords, quiet and beautiful. And then he begins to sing:

> *"I saw you dancing,*
> *You were dancing,*
> *Over the water, over the waves,*
> *And you were singing,*
> *I heard you singing,*
> *I whispered on the wind to say,*
> *Beautiful, beautiful, beautiful,*
> *So beautiful, beautiful, beautiful,*
> *Beautiful."*

I listen, carefully, trying to figure out if this is a song about Jesus, or if it's a song about somebody else, but then the song turns into a lullaby, and before I can find the words to ask, I've fallen fast asleep.

# STEP FOUR:
## INSULATE YOURSELF

I make it back to work in time for the raising of the walls.

I wouldn't have thought we could do it. There was a split second, as I stood with a few of my friends behind that first wall, when it felt as if it might tip over on us, as if the gravitational pull of the earth was too great for us to override. But we just pushed a little harder and it stood up, and other people rushed in and nailed the wall braces in place. The rest of the walls went up like that, and everything fit together like it should, and now when you look at what was once a pile of dirt and lumber, you see the skeleton of a house.

Skeletons signify death. The end. Decay. But when you stand here with your boots in the crackling grass and look at what we've built so far you see renewal. Life. About to burst forth.

# HOME

Christmas this year was unbearable.

Despite the fact that I'm currently obsessed with Christian rock anthems about loving Jesus, I've never cared much about the day of his actual birth.

Christmas in our house was always lackluster. Jane went along with the tree begrudgingly, and Tess and Rose seemed awkward accepting gifts, even when they came wrapped in Hanukkah paper. I always felt secretly annoyed with all of them at Christmastime, like if they weren't around, Dad and Cole and I could have the holly jolly Christmas you hear about in that inane song.

Christmas was the one time of year when I had a moment of wishing my family were different.

And then this year, when my terrible wish came true, I ended up feeling the absence of Jane and Tess and Rose more acutely than ever.

Things had evened out in the weeks since they'd left. Tess and I hung out at school and at parties, and we talked about many of the same things we always did: other people, and what they were doing, with whom, and how they looked while they were doing it.

I hadn't told her about what happened with Gabriel. And we didn't talk about the family, unless it was about Cole. Cole was safe territory. We loved him and his idiosyncrasies with equal devotion.

I'd seen Jane only a handful of times since our lunch at the café on Montana. There were a few times I stayed long enough at their new house to watch Jane arrive home from work, put her keys in the bowl by the front door and then kiss Cole, Tess and finally me, each on the top of the head.

I didn't know how to think of Jane, or how to explain who she was to me, and sometimes when I was with her I seemed to swallow all of my words until they sat like a brick in the bottom of my stomach, but I still loved her.

Christmas Day found me in a deep, dark funk. Cole was over at his new house in his new room with the red striped curtains. Rose was home from college and I hadn't had a chance to see her yet.

They were all together.

I was alone with Dad.

I might have called Gabriel, but he was off skiing with his perfectly intact family of four. If he'd been around I might have suggested we hang out, which probably would have led to sex, even though he was kind of going out with Sarah Denton. She was the girl he'd kiss near a keg at a party. He sometimes drove her home from school. None of this seemed to alter our encounters. They were as random and convenient as ever. They were our secret, although without the excitement that often goes along with knowing something nobody else knows. The best I can describe it is that I felt less numb when I was with Gabriel than I did when I was alone.

Dad and I went to the movies. A big-budget comedy with obvious jokes. Afterward we went out to dinner at this restaurant that's known for having the best burgers in L.A. It was strewn with white Christmas lights and mistletoe and blown-glass ornaments, and the effort they'd put into making the place feel festive put me over the edge.

I ordered a Coke. I was still drinking poison then.

"Nothing else?" Dad asked.

"Nope."

"You sure?"

"Yep."

"You okay, kiddo?" Dad cocked his head and studied me. "It'd be an understatement to point out that you seem kind of glum."

"This sucks."

He sighed. "I know it does."

"I miss them," I said.

"Me too."

"Well, then?"

He looked at me and took a long drink from his beer. "It's not that simple."

"So I've been told."

"Listen," he said, but then he stopped. I was waiting. Ready for important information to follow. But Dad just sat there.

"The Little Drummer Boy" was playing in the background for what seemed like the third time in a row. I fought off an urge to beat that Little Drummer Boy senseless with his own drumsticks.

"Do you want to know more? Should I try to explain?"

"I don't know. You're the psychiatrist. Do I want to know more?" I was extremely irritated now. With the song, with the lights, with the insufficient carbonation in my soda, with my father.

He sighed.

"You probably don't, but you deserve to know more. You aren't a child, and furthermore, you've had the misfortune of learning early that not everything works out as planned."

His voice cracked. He looked around the room.

"If you're looking to blame somebody, blame me. I wanted, so badly, to give you the kind of family you deserve, and I tried. Jane tried. But we failed. Everything just fell apart."

He paused and tried to catch my eye, but I avoided looking back at him.

"I don't want to be sitting here in this burger joint any more than you do. But the bottom line, kiddo, is that you should be worrying about your own relationships and doing your best to survive your teens. No easy feat. And I'm terribly, terribly sorry for complicating things." He reached for my hand; I pulled it back a little but then stopped. He held me by the fingertips.

"Look, I love you. Jane loves you. Tess and Rose and Cole love you. That's what matters. That's what I think. But I've already done too much talking. What do you think?"

I didn't say anything for a long, long time.

*Come, they told me, pa-rum-pa-pum-pum.*

"I think I want to go home."

# HERE

Today is the thirty-fifth annual Bailey barbecue and fireworks display.

The main drag is packed with a few too many red, white and blue sequined outfits, in my humble opinion, but I can't help appreciating the effort.

A favorite song of the L.A. bat mitzvah circuit, "Celebration," is blaring from the DJ booth.

*There's a party goin' on right he-ere*
*A celebration to last throughout the year.*

I'm singing along. I'm moving to the music. I'm even feeling a little sheepish about my khaki shorts and black tank top. Would it have killed me to wear our national colors?

People have come out in droves and they're *celebrating*, and it's great, but when I stop and think about it, I can't for the life of me understand why.

The way I see things, the people of Bailey have every reason to be angry. To feel cheated. To feel unpatriotic. To see themselves as standing alone holding the short end of the cosmic stick.

Setting aside the question of whether irresponsible human

activity is to blame for the tornado, which I still argue it is, this tornado struck Bailey at the wrong political moment.

Too soon after Katrina.

Fortunately, Homes from the Heart stepped in to help. But when the people of Bailey asked for help from the government, all they got were a few FEMA trailers and a "Hey, sorry, guys, but the hurricane kind of wiped us out."

So it would seem perfectly reasonable to me if these people didn't feel like celebrating the USA. But they're out here in red, white and blue and it dawns on me that patriotism is about much more than what your government gives you, or fails to give you, when you need it most. Patriotism is about what and who we are to each other.

And it's about disgusting food.

Take the Bailey Bun, a dessert that appears only on the Fourth of July and has made the town semifamous. It's some kind of bread stuffed with something creamy, dipped in strawberry preserves, deep-fried, then rolled in sugar, studded with raisins and put on a stick.

I don't want to seem unpatriotic, so I eat one, and I find that indeed it is just as gross as it looks.

It's a beautiful day.

Captain came in second in the hot-dog-eating contest. He was beat out by Early Joe, the town champion nine years running, who outweighs Captain by two hundred pounds.

I'm sitting in a booth with Teddy's little sisters, Alice and Grace, helping them sell lemonade and homemade cookies to raise money to rebuild the medical clinic.

Grace wanders off in an effort to round up some more customers.

"Do you like my brother?" Alice asks. She's the one in the denim sundress and red cowboy boots. Grace is the one in the baseball cap.

"Of course I do."

I stopped by the trailer the other day with Teddy to thank Diane for the peach pie, and we all sat around drinking iced tea while Grace kicked a ball back and forth with a boy half her height and Alice braided my hair. "Your hair is just like Mama's," she'd said. "You should wear it in braids."

"No, I mean do you *like* him like him?"

"You're nosy." I swat her on top of the head.

"You kno-ow," she singsongs. "Teddy had a girlfriend."

Now I'm paying attention.

"Grace really liked her, but I didn't so much. She was okay. Nice enough. But she wasn't as pretty as you."

I love this kid. She's the greatest person in the entire world.

"I don't know why they broke up. Maybe it was because she's a lesbian."

"What! Do you even know what that means?"

"Of course I do. It means that she loves other women."

"What makes you think that's what happened between Teddy and . . ."

"Amber. I saw it on TV. That's why this couple broke up on this show I watch on The N."

"Well, you watch too much TV."

"I read too."

"Good."

"And in this book I read there was a girl who broke up with her boyfriend because she was a lesbian."

"Okay, Alice. Enough. Let's sell some lemonade and get your mom's clinic rebuilt."

"Prude."

"How old are you again?"

"Ten. I'll be ten in September."

"So you're nine."

"I'm basically ten."

"Whatever you say."

Grace comes back to the booth with Teddy in tow.

"Is Alice giving you a hard time? She has a habit of asking too many questions."

Alice sticks her tongue out at him.

"Not at all. We were just having a nice little chat," I say, and she sneaks me a grin.

"Good. Now, if you two don't mind," he says to his sisters, "I'm going to steal Harper away. I know the perfect spot for watching the fireworks."

They protest. They want to come too, but he tells them they have to stay with their parents, and we walk off into the crowd.

The sun is going down and the heat is fading. At the edges, the sky is the color of a kitten's tongue. People are finding each other and walking with their folded-up blankets to the field on Bill Parson's farm.

"This way," Teddy says, and he starts walking in the opposite direction.

I take a quick look around for Marisol, Frances and Captain.

"We'll catch up with them after," he says. "C'mon."

We climb into his pickup truck, and the engine starts with a groan.

"Where are we going?"

"A little faith. That's all I ask."

"You sound like Jesus radio."

"This has nothing to do with Jesus. This is about fireworks." He pauses. "And being alone with you."

I turn to look at him, but he looks straight ahead. I don't know why I'm looking at him. If he were to turn and look at me, I'm certain I'd look away. But I'm staring at his profile, his dark curls, his eyelashes, his high cheekbones, his chin with just the smallest trace of stubble on it.

He's smiling.

"I . . . I . . ."

My heart is racing. Words are tumbling around in my head, in my throat, but I can't grab hold of them and string them together.

There's a battle going on here.

I want him. I do. I wouldn't allow myself to believe that it could come to this with Teddy, that he would want me too, that he would want to be alone with me, and yet here we are.

But I've been through this before. I've been with the boy who one minute is your friend and then, when nobody else is around, and at moments you can never anticipate, is willing to be more.

I flash forward to tomorrow. I'll be helping insulate the

walls and Teddy will be doing whatever his assignment is and I'll take a break and wander over to find him and he'll look at me blankly, and there won't be any sign, in any corner of the skeletal house, of anything having happened between us.

"I think we should go to Bill Parson's farm with everyone else," I say quietly.

He stops the truck.

"Really? Because if we go over on Stutter Road and climb the hill we can see the fireworks from the other side. We'll be closer than the farm, and higher up, so it feels like they're right in your face."

He's looking at me now. And now it's me who's looking straight ahead. It's not quite black outside, it's the deepest hue of blue, and in this light I feel lost.

"It's totally safe. I swear. I've watched from this same spot for the past few years. But if you want to go back, let's go."

"I don't know what I want."

Sometimes, when you imagine places you've never been or things you've never done, you find that the real experience isn't too far off from the one you invented in your head. Like New York. Before I ever went, I dreamed of it, and the concrete and height and glass and noise and smells of it all matched my imagination.

I pictured this summer in Tennessee for months before I came. What I imagined was heat. I imagined building strength in my biceps from operating power tools, and gaining space in my head. I pictured anonymity. I pictured no history, no present. Just work.

I didn't picture this.

A town with stories and people and fading light at the end of each day that breaks my heart. A new set of friends. Another boy. Another relationship I don't understand, with lines I can't see.

"Harper, hey, I'm sorry I said that thing about wanting to be alone with you. Maybe that sounded creepy. I don't know." He drums his fingers on the steering wheel. "I didn't mean to make any assumptions. Really, I didn't. Let's just watch some fireworks. From wherever suits you best."

I unbuckle my seat belt. I hear an explosion. At first I think it's coming from inside me, but it's not. It's in the distance. The fireworks are starting.

I slide closer to Teddy. I turn to him.

I put my hands on his shoulders. I slide them onto his bony chest.

He takes my face in his hands. He reaches back for my hair. We collide.

# HOME

One Saturday night in January, Tess invited me to sleep over at Avi's. Rose was still home from school.

One thing I'd learned about college from watching Rose go away was that you have vacations that never end. The other thing I learned was that when you go away to school, you get to start your own life, and whatever happens back at home is something that's happening to other people.

Rose seemed unfazed by the divorce. She shrugged in her typical Rose way and tossed her long dark hair to the side and said something about it being the inevitable outcome of any relationship confined by the draconian societal construct known as marriage.

"It's a prison," she said. "Eventually, the smart ones figure out how to escape."

We were sitting on the beach drinking lattes, still in our pajamas. Avi and his girlfriend, Lynn, who lived together now, had an early tennis game. It was sunny and clear and hot, too hot for a January morning. But in this new world, heat in January is a way of life.

I looked out at the ocean and the sand; I turned around and looked at Avi's condo complex and the hundreds like it up and down the coast as far as my eyes could see. I imagined it all gone, underwater, swallowed up by the rising oceans.

There was nowhere, no place, nothing, that felt safe anymore.

"Anyway, they'll be fine. It's probably better this way. They'll move on, find new lovers, have new experiences. Live their lives."

Rose seemed to have aged ten years in the five months since I'd seen her.

In high school she'd been a romantic. She pined over this gorgeous boy with dark hair, olive skin and a necklace made of white seashells who surfed and played the drums. I used to watch her get ready to go out to parties where his band, Sex Wax, would perform. Fruity-smelling skin lotions. Carefully applied eye shadow in earthy tones. Outfits assembled to appear as if they'd been thrown together.

The only thing she wanted was to be his girlfriend. For him to love her. She was never able to look at anybody else.

Then she went to college. She dated somebody her freshman year, but ever since then she'd been having only casual relationships and lots and lots of sex. She liked to talk about the liberating world of sexual encounters unadorned by any effort to define them.

I still couldn't bring myself to tell either of them that I'd been having sex with Gabriel off and on since October, encounters unadorned by any effort to define them, and that it was anything but liberating.

I didn't understand. There was Sarah Denton. There was me. Who was I to Gabriel? Were we still friends? Who was I to anyone? What had happened to all the relationships in my life that mattered?

"Tell me, Harper," Rose said. "How's Art these days?"

I looked quickly at Tess. I couldn't help it. It was our tacit agreement never to talk about Dad. I wasn't sure why I'd allowed this in the first place, but it had become a part of our new relationship.

Tess stood up and said, "I'm going in for more coffee. Anyone?"

We shook our heads.

"He's okay, I guess," I said to Rose. "He's goofier around Cole. Always trying to come up with some crazy activity for the two of them to do together when it's Cole's time at the house. Trying to be the cool dad. Other than that he's just see-ing patients, cooking barely edible meals and pestering me about my homework."

"And his love life?"

I buried my hands in the sand until they disappeared.

"I don't know. I don't really ask. If I had to guess I'd say nonexistent."

"You sure about that?"

"No, I just said I don't know. That I don't ask. Anyway, I don't see when he'd have the time."

"Oh, there's always time."

I suddenly found her college-girl wisdom intolerable and infuriating. But at the same time, I envied the distance from which she was able to view everything.

I wanted to go away. I wanted my own fresh start. My own new world where the things from home seemed smaller, like they do from an airplane window.

It would be a year and a half until I could go away to college.

But there was the summer, I thought. I'd find somewhere to go in the summer.

## HERE

When I get back to my room after being in Teddy's truck, Marisol is propped up in bed reading a magazine.

"So, how were the fireworks?" she asks.

"You saw them, didn't you?"

"Yes, *I* saw them. But the question is, did *you?*"

I smile. "Sort of."

The truth is, when I realized we were missing them I muttered something about that in between kisses, and then Teddy whispered, "Come here."

He turned his body so that he was leaning against the driver's-side door, and he stretched his leg out along the bench of the truck, and he pulled me to him so that I was leaning with my back against his chest. He covered my eyes.

"Just listen to them," he said softly in my ear. "We're not missing them at all. Fireworks have a sound that gets lost when you watch them. Just listen to the percussion. The radical rhythms. Pop-pop-poppity-pop-pop-pop. It's music."

And then he took my hair and moved it off my neck and began kissing me there and I listened to the faraway explosions.

"C'mon, Harper, don't make me sound like your mother, don't make me say something like 'Where have you been, young lady?'" Marisol says.

For a minute I freeze up inside, but then I take a breath and it melts away. Not even the mention of mothers can ruin the allover body buzz I have right now from being with Teddy.

I sit down on my bed and kick off my flip-flops.

"Okay, okay. I was with Teddy."

She jumps up. "Don't. Say. Another. Word. Not one more." She slowly opens our door and peers outside.

"I'm pretty sure the coast is clear," I say.

Linus just finished making the rounds. I caught him at the end and said, "Sorry I'm late getting back."

"Do you have a good excuse?"

When I stammered, he smiled and said, "I can see that you do. Happy Fourth of July." Then he headed toward his room.

We sneak into the hallway and tiptoe down a few doors to Frances's. Marisol taps three times.

"Yeah?" comes a quiet, almost squeaky voice.

"It's us."

The door opens and there's Captain.

"Whew. Frances is in the bathroom and I didn't know what to do."

"I totally bought you as a girl," says Marisol. "I'll double-check with Frances later, but by the sounds of things, you seem to have no balls."

He lets us inside. Frances's roommate, Liz, is gone. She's best friends with the Chicago Sisters and doesn't seem to mind crashing in their room from time to time so that Frances and Captain can have some privacy.

Frances comes out of the bathroom wearing a T-shirt of Captain's.

"What's the word?"

"Ask Harper," Marisol says.

I'm not so sure I'm up for this. I know they're just being friends, and friends want details, but I don't want to look like a total fool for sounding all romantic about my night with Teddy when tomorrow he'll ignore me and they'll all be around to watch it happen.

"What's the word, Harper?" asks Frances.

"Nothing."

"Bullshit," says Captain. "And I can prove it. Exhibit A: You were nowhere to be seen during the fireworks. Exhibit B: You have this look of happiness on your normally surly face. Exhibit C: You're here in Frances's room after lights-out, standing in the way of me getting laid. That adds up to something. So sit down and spill."

I do. I sit down and I tell them all about my magical night of listening to the fireworks with Teddy. And then I say that tomorrow it'll all be over.

"What makes you say that?" asks Marisol.

"I know certain truths about life."

"Whatever that means," says Captain. "Listen, I've seen the way he looks at you. I'm a guy, and I know certain truths too, and I know Teddy's into you. Don't forget about the pie. Guys don't bring pies to girls they aren't into. In fact, guys don't bring pies to girls, like, ever. That's kind of a sissified thing to do, but I'll let it slide 'cause I think Teddy's cool. Now, can you two get out of here so I can be alone with my hot girlfriend?"

He kisses each of us on the cheek, and so does Frances, and we say goodnight to them and tiptoe back to our room, where I go to bed and dream of invisible fireworks in an endless night sky.

* * *

When I wake up I don't remember where I am.

The room has changed shape. The bathroom entrance is on the wrong wall and my bed is facing the opposite direction. The curtains aren't right. It's too dark. The smell is off.

I sit up and shake my head, and slowly the room falls into place. Everything shifts around like pieces of an oversized jigsaw puzzle.

This isn't my room at home; it's my motel room in Tennessee. The breathing I hear coming from the other bed is Marisol. It isn't Tess.

This is now. Today.

I settle back into bed and pull up the covers. I don't want to get up.

Not just yet.

I want to remember last night and kissing Teddy. I want to hang on to these precious minutes before the day begins and I see him again and all the confusion takes hold.

We sat in his truck and he pulled me close. My face. My neck. My hair.

It's been a while. I haven't been touched like that since the last time I was with Gabriel, and that was five months ago.

Or maybe it's been never.

# HOME

It was early February. Sarah Denton was on the outs. I don't know why, because Gabriel and I never talked about Sarah

Denton, I just know that there was a party at her house and he didn't want to go. We went to a movie instead. And then back to my house.

Dad was out. It was Cole's weekend at Jane's.

Afterward we threw our clothes on and went down into the kitchen and ate pistachio ice cream. The cold stole the flush from my cheeks.

It was easy to see why Sarah Denton and all the other girls like Sarah Denton were drawn to Gabriel. He'd grown handsome. And sure of himself. He had a way of smiling and saying something playful, and with that look and those playful words he could make any awkwardness vanish.

Sometimes it was hard for me to remember the younger version of Gabriel—my friend from Mr. Ratner's math class, the movie geek with the ridiculous good-luck dance, who used to love comic-book heroes and dreamed of discovering he too had powers. Gabriel the Great, bigger and better and somehow more special than his average twelve-year-old self.

But he had finally developed a power, or at least a power over me. He had the ability to make it seem as if everything were normal. He made it seem as if there were no questions to be asked about the nature of our relationship. We were friends. Sometimes we had sex. No big deal.

I might think about asking him as we were lying there just after: *What is this? Who am I to you? Do you even want me? Could I be just anybody?*

But then he'd deliver a big smile. An inside joke. Maybe a

friendly shove. His way of saying: *See, what's so weird about any of this?* And then I'd think maybe he was right. Maybe none of those questions mattered.

In my kitchen, with the pistachio ice cream on the counter between us, I remember we talked about colleges. He was going on a trip with his father over spring break. Up and down the East Coast for interviews and tours. He wanted to go somewhere not too far outside a city. He wondered if when it came time to pack up and make the move, his car would survive the cross-country trip.

There was nothing confusing, it was just talk.

It was simple.

And it was one of the last conversations we ever had.

## HERE

Teddy is late to work.

This isn't like him. He's usually here before we arrive, but today there's no sign of him.

Of course I assume the worst. He's avoiding me.

So when I feel a tap on my shoulder and turn to find myself staring into a small bouquet of wildflowers, their stems wrapped in tinfoil, I'm so shocked I jump back, like a hornet might be hiding in there. I guess another word for what I do is *recoil*, which is not really what you want to do when the boy you're hot for hands you flowers.

I take them.

"Hey there," he says. He digs his hands into the pockets of his baggy shorts and rolls back on this heels.

"Hey there yourself," I say, and immediately wish I'd said something smarter. "You're late."

"I am."

We stare at each other. A saw grinds away in the distance.

"Well," I say, "now that we have that cleared up."

"I'm happy to see you," he blurts out.

I don't know how to do this. This isn't what I know. My limited experience with boys doesn't include what is happening right now.

But I manage a smile. And then I hand him a pencil.

"Help me measure this," I say, and we go back to work on the house that no longer looks like a skeleton. The walls are solid now.

At the end of the day he asks if we can have dinner together. I wonder briefly if this is when he's going to lay down the rules for whatever this is that's going on between us.

*I'm not your boyfriend. This doesn't mean anything.*

"Okay," I say. "Pick me up at the motel."

"Skip the bus. You don't need to change. I don't know if you've noticed, but the only restaurant in town is the Burrito Barn." He looks me up and down. Takes in my army shorts and work boots and the pink T-shirt with Mr. Bubble on the front. "Currently," he says, "you are *way* overdressed."

I get permission from Linus to skip the usual cookout by the pool, and I go tell Marisol not to save me a seat on the bus.

"Hot date with your boyfriend?"

"Don't say that."

"Why not?"

"I don't know."

"I do. You don't want me to curse it. And that's totally cool. I get it."

"Thanks."

"But I'm wondering . . . when does a guy turn from someone you're just making out with into a bona fide boyfriend?"

If I knew the answer to that question I could have spared myself months, years of confusion and angst. If I had the answer I'd bottle it and sell it and retire to a fat and happy life of doing nothing. I shrug.

"Okay," she says, and gives me a quick hug. "Have fun tonight. Remember every detail so we can overanalyze everything later when you come home."

"Okay." I smile and then turn to leave.

"And do me one more favor?"

"What?"

"Don't let whatever happened back home with that other guy mess this up with you and Teddy, okay?"

○ ○ ○

We sit outside at a picnic table. I never like eating outside in L.A., because no matter how many potted palms they surround you with, all you're doing is breathing car exhaust. But the tables here sit off the side of a totally empty road. Teddy's truck is the only vehicle in sight.

We order from a chalkboard menu, and when they call our number, which seems an odd thing to do since we're the only ones here, Teddy goes to retrieve our food.

"Madam," he says, and he bows as he puts an orange plastic tray in front of me. "Your supper has arrived."

It is hands down the worst burrito on the planet.

I gently suggest this to Teddy.

"Really? I think this place is pretty decent."

"That's obviously because you know nothing about Mexican food. Come to L.A. sometime and I'll show you *real* Mexican food." I sound like a snob. I know it, but I can't help myself.

Teddy's quiet, but that's just because he has a mouthful of burrito. He swallows and breaks into a grin.

"What? This isn't *authentic* enough for you? Is it because the chef is a little old white lady named Myrtle who's never left Bailey and has owned this place since back when it used to be known as the Burger Palace?" He wipes his mouth with a flimsy paper napkin.

"The Burger Palace?"

"Like I said, it's the only restaurant in town, and people tend to get bored."

"Look, I don't mean to rag on Myrtle but—and I'm just trying to be honest here—this burrito is abysmal. It actually makes me miss the motel food."

Teddy laughs.

"I know another place," he says. "Come on, let's go."

○ ○ ○

They're in the middle of dinner when we arrive, sitting around a plastic table under an awning in front of the trailer. Alice jumps up and gives me a hug. Grace waves and smiles at me.

"Hey, Mama," Teddy says. "Any scraps left for some hungry wanderers?"

Coach Wes, as I've taken to calling him since that's what everyone in town calls him, slaps his hands on the table. "Now, Teddy, I told you to bring her here in the first place. You know that old Myrtle Lavigne is losing her sight *and* her mind."

Diane gives Coach Wes a playful shove.

"Of course there's more food, honey. Have a seat." She gets up and goes into the trailer and comes back with cold cucumber soup, corn bread and grilled chicken.

"Were you guys on a date?" Alice asks.

I go red. The kid is fearless.

I busy myself with my soup.

"Hush now," says Coach Wes.

"But Daddy, I—"

"I said hush."

The dinner is delicious, and afterward I help Diane do the dishes over her strenuous objection. There's barely room for the two of us in the kitchen. I dance around her, careful that we don't crash into each other.

The kitchen is also the dining area, but it wouldn't be able to hold the whole family. It opens onto a small living room, where Teddy spends his nights on the couch.

Coach Wes and Diane sleep in one tiny room and Alice and Grace share the other.

As Diane hands me glasses and I dry them with a red-checkered cloth, I do some snooping. There's a poster of Miles Davis taped to the wall. A few photographs on the shelf: Coach Wes with his football team. A shorter Teddy with bigger hair and the twins without their front teeth. An older couple I don't recognize. That's about it.

I rub my hand along the armrest of the couch like I might be able to learn more about Teddy by touching the place where he goes to sleep at night.

I know so little about him.

I know that he graduated in June with the sun lighting up the school gym. I know that he got into the University of Texas in Austin (which he says has a killer music scene) but deferred. He wants to stay in Bailey and help rebuild the medical clinic. I know that he works hard. That he doesn't goof off at the site like the rest of us do. I know that I love kissing him.

I hand the dried glasses back to Diane. She puts them in the cupboard. I hear Teddy's voice coming in through the open front door, followed by laughter. Big laughter.

What makes him laugh like that?

···

The conversation doesn't happen, no talk of what we aren't and what we cannot be. Ground rules are not set.

Just more kissing in the truck before he drops me home, back at my motel.

## HOME

It was the party of the year. Presidents' Day weekend. Sabrina Christiansen's parents were in Switzerland. She hired a DJ.

Sabrina Christiansen lives in a Bel Air mansion that used to be owned by Mickey Rooney. He's this short, old bald guy who was once a famous movie star.

She has a pool and a tennis court and a pool house and probably even another house to go with the tennis court, but I never got that far.

I almost didn't go.

Dad and I had a monster fight. He had something important that night and couldn't find a babysitter for Cole. I told him I had something important too: Sabrina Christiansen's party. He told me I went to parties every weekend. It wouldn't kill me to skip one. I told him he didn't understand. He told me I was being a drama queen.

You get the picture.

So I sulked and barely said a word to Dad for the two days leading up to the party and I made no plans to go with anyone.

Then Saturday night rolled around and Dad surprised me with the news that he'd found someone who could watch Cole. It turned out he'd been making all kinds of calls in the pursuit of a trustworthy babysitter, and one finally came through at the last minute.

I threw my arms around him and told him I loved him.

He said, "I love you too, you selfish brat."

I drove alone. The rumor that there would be valet parking turned out not to be true, and I had to walk up a winding road with old-fashioned streetlamps.

The moon was full.

I ran into Natalie Banks as I was getting out of my car and we made the hike together, which was tougher on her because of her stiletto-heeled boots.

We'd been in school together since kindergarten, but we'd never been more than casual friends. That didn't mean I didn't know things about her or that she didn't know things about me. I knew that Natalie was on the volleyball team, that her father lived in England and that she'd lost her virginity to Dixon Michaels in the summer between eighth and ninth grade.

"Where's Tess?" she asked.

So maybe Natalie didn't know things about me.

Or maybe news of my family's implosion wasn't nearly as big as I'd thought.

Or maybe she was some kind of diabolical she-devil who thrived on other people's discomfort.

Or, to not assume the worst, maybe Natalie figured Tess and I were getting through all this with our friendship intact.

"I'm not sure," I said. "Probably at the party already. Probably by the keg. Probably being circled by ten different guys."

This was true about Tess. She drew tons of attention at parties. It had something to do with the confidence she'd pick up after a drink or two. The hot outfits she put together probably didn't hurt either.

Tess was a master flirt who rarely followed through. She liked to be courted. The only boys she'd ever fooled around with were ones who had pursued her for weeks. She was slow and careful, and this made what happened at Sabrina Christiansen's party all the more shocking.

I didn't see her anywhere. After the first hour I figured she'd skipped the party. Maybe she had plans that night with Jane.

I drank flat beer. I talked more with Natalie and this guy Ben who was in my history class. The DJ was playing eighties music, but I'm not much of a dancer.

I walked down to the pool where people sat dangling their feet, and watched how the shimmering pool light made their faces look tanned and their teeth ultrawhite. I looked in the pool house, where the stoners were camped out doing bong hits.

I wandered over to the tennis court. It was dark.

I didn't notice the couple making out in the grass just off the foul line until I almost tripped over them.

And then they looked up at me. And the full moon lit their faces.

Tess and Gabriel.

# STEP FIVE:
# WINDOWS AND DOORS

Teddy and I are westbound on I-40.

We're rocking out to the sound of some new Jesus band. There's an urgency to their love: Enthusiasm spills out like the drawing of a child who can't keep his markers inside the lines.

It's Saturday. It's hot and the air conditioner is straining the engine of Teddy's truck. He's wearing a black baseball cap and a white T-shirt and his hand is on my knee.

This past week I partnered with Marisol. On Monday she smashed her thumb with a hammer, so she spent the rest of the week with it wrapped in a white gauze bandage, sitting off to the side, watching me work and distracting me with her constant chattering.

Yesterday we anchored the back door. We needed Linus's

help because Marisol is pretty much useless. And also, doors are heavy.

The door came prehung with jambs, a threshold and exterior trim, but we, or more accurately *I*, had to flash the doorsill before we could fit the door to the frame of the house. Proper flashing keeps out water and rot.

I still can't believe I know how to flash a doorsill. Me. I know how to flash a doorsill. Go figure.

When I finished we called Linus over to help us lift the door into place and he commented on my expert flashing. Felt along the sides and the top, aluminum on the bottom.

"Excellent work," he said as he smoothed his hands up and down the felt.

"Thank you," said Marisol.

I glared at her.

"Well, I told you when it looked crooked, didn't I?"

I turned to Linus. "Marisol's using her minor thumb injury as a way of avoiding doing any real work."

"Harper's using the bad luck of prior relationships to avoid accepting that she's crazy in love with Teddy," she shot back.

I shoved her.

"Ow," she said. "Careful of my thumb."

Linus smiled at us both.

"He's a nice boy," he said.

Today this nice boy is taking me to Graceland.

I've never been much of an Elvis fan. Though I can hum a few bars of "Hound Dog" and "Blue Suede Shoes."

"Remind me why we're doing this?" I ask Teddy.

"Because if we don't, you'll spend the rest of your life explaining how you could have spent a summer in a small town about an hour outside of Memphis and never gone to Graceland."

We were going to borrow Coach Wes's car so we could take Marisol, Captain and Frances, but then Frances woke up with the flu, and Captain wanted to stay and take care of her, and Marisol didn't want to be the third wheel. I told her that was ridiculous, but she still refused, and now I'm alone with Teddy.

Graceland is a place for Elvis fanatics. Here you'll find every detail about the King and his transformation from an eager, pretty-faced mama's boy with a cheap guitar and self-conscious leg twitch, into a bejeweled, jumpsuit-wearing hedonist who looked like he'd been inflated with a bicycle pump.

Graceland is both bigger and smaller than I imagined it.

The mansion itself isn't all that impressive from the outside. There are much, much larger houses all over Los Angeles. About ten Gracelands could fit into one of Sabrina Christiansen's mansions.

Graceland is all about the inside, about Elvis's over-the-top decor. Stained-glass peacock windows, a fifteen-foot-long sofa, a television room with three screens and blue and gold lightning bolts on the wall, the poolroom covered in tapestry, the jungle room with a green shag-carpeted ceiling.

When you walk out of the house at the end of the tour and you look back at it, you'd swear it's an optical illusion.

It feels much larger than it looks, but that's because he filled the place up with his gigantic personality.

Graceland is a cartoon. A bad joke. At least that's how it feels to me after weeks of contemplating the simplest things a house needs: a room for cooking, a room for sitting, some rooms for sleeping. A tornado-safe room to run to. A place to live that's rooted to the ground and won't get hauled away when your FEMA grant runs out.

We share one of Elvis's favorite fried-banana and peanut-butter sandwiches before getting back in the truck and heading into the city.

We park downtown and take a long, lazy late-afternoon walk. We pass the Lorraine Motel where Martin Luther King, Jr., was assassinated, which is now the National Civil Rights Museum.

We walk up a pedestrian street with a trolley that runs down its center. Beautiful old brick buildings crowd next to each other, many with empty storefronts.

There aren't any people around. Maybe it's the heat. Or maybe they've all gone somewhere else. Moved on. Used up all this city had to offer.

We walk down to the banks of the Mississippi River and sit. The grass is tall. Bugs are circling us.

I remember learning to spell Mississippi.

*Mi-ssi-ssi-ppi.*

"A kid died jumping in right here on a dare last August," Teddy says, and shakes his head. "It doesn't look like it, but there can be a mean undercurrent."

The Mississippi River.

It never sounded real. I couldn't imagine something dividing this gigantic country in two. But here it is, muddy and brown. It isn't even all that wide. I can see the edges of Arkansas. If we drove up and over the bridge, we'd be there in a matter of minutes. It's a Saturday and there's no traffic.

Somewhere beyond those edges of Arkansas is my home. If I could see forever, I'd be able to see its white trim and red door. I could see Dad sitting in the kitchen. Cole's toys on the floor. Tess's empty bed.

But it feels like I could never cross this river, even if I had an entire lifetime in which to do it. In some ways I'm farther away from home than I've ever been. An imaginary divider has gone up, splitting this country and my life in two, bigger and wider and stronger than the Mississippi.

And I can't get back to the other side because I can't climb something that can't be climbed or swim across something that can't be survived on a dare.

○ ○ ○

Now I understand where all the people went: Beale Street.

Teddy takes my hand. It's the first time I've ever walked down a street holding the hand of someone who is not my parent.

It's only a little past four in the afternoon, but already people are stumbling around drunk, spilling neon-colored frozen alcoholic sludge from their forty-two-ounce plastic cups. The clubs are packed. Blues music falls out one door, country out another. From a courtyard I hear a really bad reggae version of "Piece of My Heart" by Janis Joplin.

Teddy leans over and shouts in my ear, "So *whaddya think?*"

What am I supposed to say? I hate it here. It's loud and bright and hot, and it feels totally phony, like we're at the Disneyland version of Memphis. The people here could vomit at any minute, and the cops on horseback look really mean.

"*Isn't it awful?*" he shouts.

I look around and suddenly everything's perfect. I want to find a postcard, a T-shirt, some memento of this spot and this moment.

We walk off the main strip and wind our way along a few tree-lined blocks until we come to a little restaurant on a corner. He holds open the door for me.

We slide into a booth of blue and white vinyl.

It's dark and cool. The walls are wood paneled and covered with old black-and-white photographs. Sawdust lines the floor. There's a small stage with a piano, a stand-up bass and a drum kit at the far end of the restaurant.

A large black woman with dangling gold earrings and an apron comes over to greet us.

"Welcome to Alicia's. Y'all hungry?"

"Yes, ma'am," says Teddy.

"All right then," she says with a smile, and walks off.

"Um," I say, "are we going to order?"

"We just did," he says. "She'll bring us whatever she's cooking today, and trust me, it's going to knock your socks off." He rubs his hands together.

"Even better than the Burrito Barn?"

"Even better than the Burrito Barn." He smiles. He gestures to the stage. "The music'll start around six-thirty or so, and until then, we're going to sit here and eat some killer food, and you're going to tell me everything I need to know about you."

"Okay, well, for starters, I hate talking about myself."

"Tell me something I don't know."

It's quiet in here. Hushed conversations. It feels like secrets are hanging from the coatrack.

Before I stop to think I blurt out, "I'm not a virgin."

"Okay," he says. "I guess that's getting right to the heart of things."

"I'm not sure why I just told you that."

"Because it's important. I'm glad you did. For the record, I'm not either."

"Amber?" I ask.

"How'd you know that?"

I give him a look that says, *How do you think I know?*

"Ahhh," he says. "Alice."

I nod.

"And you? Gabriel, right?"

How does he know? I certainly never said anything about Gabriel to bigmouth Alice.

"Captain," he says. "I had to do a little background

research before getting up the courage to put the moves on you."

I smile.

"Is everything over with him?" he asks. "Or is he wasting his summer on one of those famous California beaches waiting for you to come home?"

"I don't even think he knows I'm here."

"So then it's over."

"It never really began."

"What happened?"

"That's a long story."

"We've got until six-thirty," he says. "Then the band comes in and musicians don't like it much when people talk through their set."

Alicia brings us two glasses of water and a basket of corn muffins.

"How 'bout a shot of Jack Daniel's?" Teddy asks her.

She laughs. "How 'bout you grow up a few good years," she says, and walks away.

He smiles at me. "Can't hurt to try." He takes a sip of his water. "So tell me about this Gabriel person."

"Why don't you tell me about Amber first."

"Oh, I don't know. She was okay. I don't think her daddy liked me much, so we didn't spend time around her place. We were together at school. And we went to parties. She introduced me to Jack Daniel's." He smiles and nods toward the bar. "I guess it seemed fine to be with her when all that high school stuff mattered to me. After the tornado, things changed. I didn't care about parties. Or the prom. And she didn't like that I didn't care. Not that I really blame her. She's entitled to her last months of high school being carefree and fun. I just wasn't the fun kind of boyfriend anymore."

I reach across the table and take his hand. I notice for the first time that he bites his fingernails.

"She's going to school next year in Alabama, where she can't wait to pledge a sorority. Her birthday is in February and she's allergic to shellfish. Okay. That's enough about her. Tell me about Gabriel."

"I don't really know where to start. We're friends. Or we were. But we were also more. It never quite felt right between us. And then it just felt plain miserable when Tess entered the picture."

"Your sister?"

"Well, she's kind of my sister. Or she was. See? I told you it's a long story."

"So get talking."

I tell him everything. I go back to what I told him that day by the pool, when he brought me the pie, but this time I don't leave anything out. I tell him about how my real mother died when I was two. I tell him about Jane and the June Gloom picnic at the beach when we first met and how Tess and I grew up sharing a room and sharing clothes and how now we barely speak. I tell him about the hand-to-breast incident of eighth grade and the teary back rub Gabriel gave me after Tess moved out and how that turned into more. I tell him about my dad and what Tess finally told me about him and why she wouldn't go near our house anymore.

# HOME

I ran away.

I ran from the tennis courts, back past the pool house, up the lawn, through Sabrina Christiansen's mansion and down the winding streets sardined with fancy cars.

I climbed in my front seat and sat. I had my hands on the steering wheel, but I didn't put the key into the ignition.

There was a knock at the passenger window.

Tess's face looked lovelier than ever. Her cheeks were flushed. (Were they flushed from chasing me down or from whatever it was she had been doing with Gabriel?) Her hair was in a loose ponytail. Her shirt was Indian print, billowing, with open buttons at the top through which you could see her freckled chest.

She climbed into the car.

"You look really pissed off."

"How . . . how . . . how could you?"

"I thought things were just casual with you and Gabriel. And anyway, I thought they were over. I mean, he was going out with Sarah Denton and you didn't seem to care."

"Well, things weren't over. And they weren't casual."

"Shit, Harper. How am I supposed to know that? Really?

How am I supposed to know about what's happening in your life when you never tell me anything?"

"And that's *my* fault?"

"It sort of is, yes."

"You're a bitch."

I'd never talked to Tess like that before. At that moment in my car, with me behind the steering wheel and Tess with her mouth hanging open, something occurred to me for the very first time.

Things were never equal with Tess.

Despite my being only a few weeks younger, she dominated me like an older sister. I always let her take the lead, or maybe it was that she always took it without ever giving me a chance to get there first.

When we played cards as children she'd make up new rules and I'd let her, and it didn't even bother me that the rules always tipped in her favor.

That was just what she was doing now. She'd been doing it since October.

Making up new rules.

Creating a game in which her home was safe and mine dangerous. Her mother was good and my father bad. And as usual, I'd accepted everything like the timid younger sister.

And tonight in my car, she was constructing yet another set of the Rules According to Tess. In this game there was nothing wrong with what Tess was doing by the tennis court with Gabriel, and I was overreacting by calling her a bitch.

"Get out of my car."

"Get over yourself. So I made out with Gabriel. So what? It's stupid. I'm not committing any cardinal sin here. I'm not violating any laws or breaking any vows, which is more than I can say for your father."

"What? What exactly are you trying to say?"

"Exactly what I'm trying to say, no, what I'm saying, is that your dad is a sleaze, and after everything he did, Mom still wants me to protect him by keeping my mouth shut around you. But now I don't care because you're sitting there with that look on your face like *I'm* the one who did something terrible, but all I did was kiss some guy at a party who isn't even your boyfriend, while your dad fucked one of his patients' mother while he was married to mine."

She got out and slammed the door.

I thought the window might shatter, but it didn't. The full moon slipped behind a cloud. The only thing left was the sound of glass not breaking.

# HERE

I don't ride the bus to the work site anymore. Teddy picks me up in the mornings and he brings me a real cup of coffee in my travel mug. Yesterday he came early and we went back for breakfast to his trailer, where Diane made us egg and sausage sandwiches on biscuits and Coach Wes asked us questions about *To Kill a Mockingbird*, which he was in the middle of reteaching to his summer-school class.

"Your parents are the best. You're so lucky," I said to Teddy as we walked up the hill to the site.

"You just say that 'cause you don't have to live with them," he said. "They can be just as annoying as anyone's parents."

"Like how?"

"Well, my mom's a mom. You know. She can be a nag. She babies my sisters. She thinks hip-hop is the work of the devil. Really. She does. But I just tell her that she'll never understand black music. That really infuriates her. And Dad's obsessed with football season. You should be here in the fall. He becomes a totally different person. He can't talk about anything else. We have football players over all the time and Mom has to cook these huge meals, after a full day's work at the clinic, and I don't think she really likes it and Dad doesn't seem to notice or care one way or the other." He stopped in his tracks and looked at me. "Is this too much information?"

I took his hand. "When it comes to you and your family, there's no such thing as too much information."

○ ○ ○

This morning we're eating with the others in the conference room of the motel: Raisin Bran out of a plastic bowl, and a too-ripe banana.

Frances is mad at Captain because he got a letter from his ex-girlfriend that borders on X-rated, with visuals included in the form of a Polaroid.

Captain seems to be loving every minute of Frances's tantrum. Usually she keeps things pretty close to the vest. Captain tends to be the one who shows all the emotion and Frances, with her too-cool New York attitude, acts like she barely tolerates him. But this morning her sulkiness reveals everything.

"C'mon, baby," he pleads with a troublemaker's grin. He takes the picture out of his back pocket and holds it out toward Frances. "Look. She's not even *that* hot. I mean, those tan lines are too damn much. I'm so over the Florida look. I like my girl to be all pasty-fleshed, like you." He reaches for her but she pulls away.

"Dude," says Teddy. "You should really shut up. I think you're kind of blowing this."

Captain tosses the picture onto the table.

Teddy scoops it up and stares at it for a long time. Then he peers over the top of it at me. "She's nothing special."

That's a lie. I've seen the picture. If I could cut and paste my own body from an assortment of perfect physical features, it would look exactly like hers. And now that Teddy is staring at it, and comparing it to what I'm stuck with, I feel slightly ill.

"I'm about to do you a big favor," Teddy says to Captain, and he gets up and flings the Polaroid into the trash can.

Captain shoots Frances a smile as he brushes his shaggy hair off his forehead. "See, baby? See what I do for you?"

She stands up and pushes in her chair. "You didn't do shit, Captain. Teddy did it." And she storms out of the room.

Captain shrugs at Teddy and then gets up and goes after her. "But, baby . . ."

"Well, I'm going back to finish packing," Marisol says.

It's her father's sixtieth birthday this weekend, and there's some kind of family reunion. Her parents made special arrangements to fly her home. She's thrilled. Not so much about the family reunion. It's all about seeing Pierre.

She'll be gone for three nights. We talked about what might happen with Teddy and me when I have the room to myself.

"Is this when you guys start having sex? Help me here, I don't know how this works."

"You mean, you and Pierre . . ."

"Nope." She shook her head. "Whenever I think about it—and believe me, the thought crosses my mind, like, a lot—I picture Sister Jean."

"Who's that?"

"She's this stern and rather unattractive nun at my school. She's got a butt as wide as a Buick. I plan to keep this image handy till I'm married."

"And Pierre is cool with this?"

"I'm not sure he gets Sister Jean's role in everything, but he's okay with waiting. He's the rare breed of guy equipped with preternatural patience."

We never got any further on the topic of what would happen with Teddy. Topic avoided. Score one for me.

Now Marisol gets up from the table and gives us each a hug.

"So, I'll see you two in a few days. I'll be gone. You'll have the room to yourselves." She gives me a final pat on the shoulder. "Good luck with that."

Teddy and I are alone. An awkward silence takes over as the things we haven't talked about pile up between us on the table.

He's seen Captain's ex-girlfriend's naked body, but he hasn't seen mine. We haven't done more than kiss. I share a room with Marisol and he lives in a tiny trailer with his parents and his twin sisters, one of whom is the nosiest child on earth.

You do the math.

And honestly, I'm afraid. All I know so far is that having sex does nothing to further a relationship. It only complicates things.

But with Marisol leaving for three nights, I'm thinking there's no avoiding it, so maybe I should bring it up.

But I don't know how.

Gabriel and I never talked about having sex. Ever. It just happened, I never knew why it would one night and why it wouldn't the next. After that first time it seemed always to be up to him, and when it was over, he'd act like nothing had happened, and so sometimes it felt like, well, *nothing*.

And other times it felt like everything.

Teddy moves his chair closer to mine. "I've been thinking about something."

But I guess I don't have to bring up the question of sex. Teddy will. He's a guy. All guys ever think about is sex. And

Teddy's enough of a grown-up to think about it *and* talk about it.

"What have you been thinking about?"

"My aunt Abigail."

Never, in a million years, would I have guessed that these would be the words that would come out of his mouth right now.

"What about your aunt Abigail?"

"She's my mother's sister, but I've never met her. My mother doesn't speak to her and hasn't for twenty-two years. The truth is, I don't even know if she's alive or where she is, because my mom's parents are dead, so there isn't any tie left to her. The point is, she's my mom's sister, and they used to be pretty close when they were kids, and now they don't know each other anymore."

"What happened?"

"When my mom met my dad and they fell in love, she didn't have the greatest reaction to a black man dating her sister and Mom never forgave her for that."

"That sounds reasonable."

"Does it?"

"It does to me."

"I don't know. . . . I mean, sure, obviously racism is inexcusable, and I certainly don't mean to be apologizing for it, but maybe it's something she would have gotten over. Maybe if Abigail had gotten to know Dad, and realized he's just Dad, then maybe there'd be that much less racism in the world. Anyway, what I'm really trying to say is that Mom lost a sister, and she didn't even put up a good fight. I've watched her be sad her whole life because of that. She has a hole in her nobody can fill. And now it's just too late."

Talking about sex would have been less confusing for me than figuring out how to respond to this story.

I'm quiet for a long time.

"Tess did things to hurt me," I finally say.

"Maybe that's because she was hurting too."

He slides his chair even closer and puts his arms around my waist. "You need to fix this."

I stare at the planes of his face. His lips. A small cluster of freckles near his left eye.

"You're not normal," I say.

"Normal's overrated."

"How come you're not trying to figure out how to get me to let you crash in my room for the next few nights?"

"Oh, I already have that covered." He pulls me even closer.

"You do?"

"Yeah." He kisses me just above my ear.

"So what's your plan?"

"I'm just going to ask, like a good Southern boy," he whispers in my ear. "Real nice and polite-like."

# HOME

When I came back that night, Dad was still out. Cole was asleep. I paid the babysitter from the rolled-up wad of bills we kept in the drawer with the tinfoil and plastic bags. I opened the refrigerator and stood there, letting the cold escape onto my face and into my lungs. I went and sat at the counter. Pavlov curled himself at my feet.

I waited for what felt like a long time.

Dad's key in the front door made Pavlov's ears stand up, but the footfalls were Dad's, so he settled back down to sleep.

"Hi, honey."

There was Dad, facing me, his keys still in his hand.

"What's wrong?"

Here we were. Back in the kitchen. Just like we were months earlier. But this time he was standing and I was sitting. And this time *I* was about to surprise *him*.

"Tell me about what happened."

"What do you mean?"

"You know what I mean," I said, and I looked at him, hard. His face fell and he put his keys on the counter.

"I'm an asshole," he said. "That's what happened." He pulled a stool around and sat down facing me.

If he was looking for me to contradict him, he was looking in the wrong place.

"Go on."

"I've screwed up everything. Everything. I've even screwed this up, right here. This isn't how we should be having this conversation. You shouldn't be coming to me with this. I should have just told you."

"Told me what?"

"Told you . . ."

"That you had an affair?"

"Yes."

"With your patient's mother? Isn't that just a little unethical?"

He winced like he'd just been bitten on the face.

"Yes. It is."

I tried to calculate how many minutes, hours, days I'd spent feeling sorry for Dad. How I tried to wish his dark circles away. The hair back on his head. The pounds back on his disappearing frame.

I was trying to work up some anger. But when I reached for it, I grasped only air.

I thought of this picture I have of Dad and me when I'm about three. We were at a party for a college friend of his where children probably weren't welcome, but in those years Dad never went anywhere without me. I'm in his lap and he's clutching me around my waist.

That picture always confused me. From one angle it's sad: Here's this man who's lost and has nobody in the world but this three-year-old with a sour expression, tangled hair and a shirt that clashes with her pants. From another angle, it's beautiful: Here's this man and this child who have each other to cling to through whatever the world can conjure up.

Dad is all I have.

"I really thought you loved her."

"It's so much more complicated than that, Harper. Of course I loved Jane. I do love Jane. I wish things were that simple. I wish it were as simple as having an affair. An affair isn't everything, you know. It's just one small part of a much more complicated picture."

"So are you still with the patient's mother?"

"I wasn't ever 'with' her."

"Explain that one, Dad."

"I'd rather not."

"I bet."

He reached for my hand but I yanked it away.

"Look, like I said, an affair isn't everything. It's more like a symptom."

I felt totally and completely exhausted. I rubbed my eyes. "I don't get it."

"I don't expect you to." He attempted a weary smile. "Give yourself a break. Don't try to figure everything out. I know it's your impulse, but fight it."

I scratched with my fingernail at a dirty spot between the tiles on the counter, not wanting to look at Dad. Not knowing where to look.

"Also, I'm not too keen on you figuring out that I'm a terribly flawed human being." He paused until I lifted my eyes to meet his. "I much prefer being Superdad."

I stood up to go to my room, but then suddenly I was moving toward my father, and collapsing into him like a child, crying tears stored up from everything that had happened that night, and over the past weeks, and months, and years of my life.

# HERE

Right before Teddy's due to pick me up for dinner, there's a knock on my door.

Seth. He tells me I have a call on the pay phone in the hallway, and then stretches his neck to see beyond me into my empty room.

"She's gone, Seth. She went home to visit her *boyfriend*."

"Oh, right." He stands in front of me, dejected.

So it's finally taken this, *me* boyfriending Seth, for the reality of Pierre to sink in. I feel bad for him. Big, bulky Seth suddenly looks so small standing in my doorway. I put a hand on his shoulder and give it a squeeze.

"She'll be back in a few days, you know, and when she's back you should come by and hang out." I can almost feel Marisol's elbow in my ribs even though she's half a continent away, but I can't help it. I just can't stand Seth's look of crushed hope.

I assume it's Teddy calling to tell me he's running late. He's the only one who ever calls me here. I call Dad on Sundays; he never calls me.

I pick up the phone. "Is this a formal affair, or will cargo pants and a tank top do?"

"I have absolutely no idea, but my general philosophy about such things is that it's always better to be overdressed than underdressed."

"Jane?"

"Hi, Harper. Is the tank top a spaghetti-strap number, or are we talking wifebeater? It makes all the difference."

I'm caught completely off guard. It's like I'm listening to a voice from beyond, and what I learn standing with my mouth hanging open in the motel hallway is that when talking to the ghost of someone you used to know, it takes a while to find the right words.

All I can come up with is: "How are you?"

"That's what I called to ask you."

"I'm fine."

"Just fine?"

"Better than fine, I guess."

"Sounds like it. At least you're off to an event of some kind at which a tank top may not be suitable. I'm looking ahead to a night in my pajamas eating frozen enchiladas."

"Where is everyone?"

"Cole's with your dad. Rose went on a road trip to visit a boy from school who lives in Chicago. She's driving that old station wagon with a friend, but she may be stuck in Colorado and I'd never know because she doesn't bother to call."

There's a pause during which Jane seems to take a sip of something hot.

I manage to ask, "And Tess?"

"She's working at this restaurant in Malibu. It's really more like a diner, complete with a fifties motif, but the burgers cost fifteen dollars, so I refuse to call it a diner. She's on the two-to-eleven shift."

"Oh."

"You should give her a call. At the very least to tease her about her uniform."

"Sure. Maybe."

"She misses you."

My skin itches. My mouth is dry. I want to get off the phone. I need to get off the phone.

"I know it's not really my place, Harper, but I thought it important that you know that. If she won't tell you, I will. She misses you. And by the way, I miss you too."

Just as I'm about to disappear into a wordless hole, a dark place of grief and longing, Teddy rounds the corner and smiles broadly at me.

I stand up straight. Words come.

"I've got to go, Jane. Thanks for everything."

"I just thought you should know."

"I mean, thanks for being my mother."

"I'm not done with that part yet, I hope."

"Good."

I put the phone back into its cradle as Teddy reaches out and grabs me around my waist.

○  ○  ○

A heavy thunderstorm struck this afternoon and the ground is wet. The cicadas have quieted down and there's a pleasant breeze outside. Alice and Grace made colorful paper lanterns and Coach Wes helped hang them this afternoon. The light they cast is lovely. It's like eating at a tropical cantina.

Diane has prepared another of her fantastic meals. We hold hands while Coach Wes says grace. The Wrights do this every time they sit down to eat and I've come to sort of enjoy it. I hold Teddy's hand in front of the world. I pause and appreciate what it feels like to sit down to a home-cooked meal with a family.

Tonight Coach Wes says, "Father, thank you for this bounty of food and love and for the young people around this great country who stepped out of their lives to help rebuild ours. And thank you for introducing Harper into our home, may she keep that crazy smile on our Teddy's homely face. Amen."

"Amen."

I'm a wreck all through dinner. All I can think about is tonight. My anonymous room of polyester curtains and tacky art, with Teddy in it. The hours we'll fill together. I hardly eat a thing. Coach Wes takes notice.

"What's the matter, Harper, don't you like my wife's cooking?"

"No . . . it's not that, it's just that I had a big lunch."

"Diane doesn't take kindly to folks not eating her food. You better at least hide something in your napkin."

"Wes! Leave the poor girl alone. Something's bothering her and she doesn't have much of an appetite, that's all."

My face is flushing.

"What's wrong?" asks Alice. "Is it Teddy? What did he do? You can tell me. I won't tell anyone."

"Go on," says Diane. "Tell her. Alice is a wonderful keeper of secrets."

"There's something called boundaries, everybody." Teddy lays his palms flat on the table. "You should really look into them."

"All right, all right, I'll eat!" I say.

They all cheer. I'm suddenly at ease. Teddy gives me a radiant smile and a look passes between us. It feels as if we've been exchanging glances filled with understanding forever.

We have dessert and mint tea. Alice and Grace tell stories from camp. Diane talks about the temporary clinic. Today she saw a man from one of the other local building projects with a nail through his thumb. She shakes her fork at Teddy and me and tells us we should always pay careful attention when we're working on the house, especially when using the nail gun.

Teddy brings out his guitar and sings a blues song, something about his baby who done him wrong, and Diane harmonizes, and a few neighbors gather around to listen.

After the table is cleared I take a walk with the twins so they can show me a fort they've been building in a patch of trees on the property.

I expect to see a sheet serving as the roof and some branches for walls and maybe an old piece of carpeting for the floor, like the kinds of forts Tess and I used to build in the backyard. But instead what they lead me to is a beautiful little house, painted bright pink, with four walls and a roof and a plywood door on hinges and a cutout square for a window. It's just big enough to fit both girls and a small child-sized table and chairs.

"How did you guys build this? It's amazing."

"Teddy helped us," they say in unison.

"And some guy with a red beard," adds Grace.

"Linus," I say, and I give the walls a shake.

Solid as anything.

We walk back to the trailer and I hug Teddy's family good-night. We climb into the truck. We turn onto the dark road, damp gravel crunching underneath the tires. My room is empty. I tidied it this afternoon for Teddy.

I'm not a tidier.

We stop at the intersection with the road to the motel. Teddy flips on his left-turn blinker even though there's no other car in sight. The click-clacks rattle the silence of the cab. He lifts his foot off the brake and makes the turn.

"Listen," says Teddy, and he pops a tape into the tape deck.

I stare at it. "A tape deck? I thought these things were an urban legend."

"It's an old truck. Not the point here." He adjusts the volume. "I want you to hear something."

A few notes plucked on a guitar and then a voice comes in:

*I saw you dancing,*
*You were dancing,*
*Over the water, over the waves . . .*

"Hey, this is the song you sang on the pie night."

"The pie night?"

"Yeah, that's how I think of it. The pie night. The night you came to my room and brought Jack Daniel's and ate pie and played this song on the guitar. I thought you wrote this."

"No. I may be cool, but I'm not that cool."

"It's beautiful."

"It's country music, baby."

"No way."

"Way."

We listen in silence for a minute. I thought country music was all twangy guitar and do-si-do-your-partner. I never knew it could be like this.

Teddy reaches over and slides me closer to him. "Every time I hear this song now I think of you. I go around humming it in my head all the time. All day long. It's like a mantra."

"Everyone has a mantra but me."

"What?"

"Nothing."

The song ends and Teddy pops the tape out.

"See? I'm trying to be all romantic and you're busy dogging my tape deck."

"You're right. Sorry." I run my hand over the part of the dashboard with the tape deck in it. "You know—" My throat catches and I clear it. "I've always wanted there to be a song that made somebody think of me."

We're parked in front of the motel. He leans in and we kiss. He holds my face in his hands.

"I don't know how to do this," I say in an almost-whisper.

"It's easy. You pull on the handle in one smooth motion, you push the door away from you."

"No. I mean, I don't know how to sneak you in, and what to say to Linus when he knocks for lights-out, or how to face your parents."

"Harper—"

I put up a hand to indicate I'm not finished yet.

"I don't know how to do this. I don't know how to be with you tomorrow. I don't know how to have a relationship that means anything. I don't know how to have somebody want to be with me. I don't know how I'm going to pack my bags at the end of this summer and go back to my other life."

He grabs both of my hands and moves his face closer to mine so that I can't do anything but look back at him.

"Why don't we just hang out?"

"Hang out?"

"Yes. We'll just hang out tonight. That's it. I promise."

This turns out to be a lie too, but it's the kind of lie that's easy to forgive.

# HOME

At least Gabriel tried to explain himself, which is more than can be said for Tess. He cornered me in the parking lot before school started Monday morning.

"I tried calling you all weekend."

I kept walking.

"Why are you ignoring me?"

I picked up the pace.

"We were just making out. So what?"

I thought I'd look like an idiot if I started running, so instead I walked as fast as I could, and it looked like that crazy power walk you see middle-aged Beverly Hills women doing in their velour sweat suits, with huge swinging arm motions, so I ended up looking like a bigger idiot than if I'd just taken off at full speed.

"Harper, c'mon."

Gabriel dropped a book, bent down to get it and then had to sprint to catch up.

"It's not like we're going out or anything. We're friends. We're old friends."

I stopped, pivoted and stared at him.

Finally. He'd defined us.

A list of responses shuffled around in my head. There were so many to choose from, but I knew, somehow, that I'd never be able to say the right thing. So instead I shook my head, and turned back around, and walked slowly up the steps to the school entrance, and Gabriel let me go.

Tess and I went the entire week without running into each other. She very carefully and successfully avoided me. A few times I saw her disappear around a corner or duck into a classroom.

When she got out of the car and slammed my door the night of the party she, like she always did, got the last word. *She* was the one who got to make the angry, dramatic exit. *She* made it seem like *I'd* done something wrong, when *I* deserved the last word. *I* deserved to be the one who slammed doors and didn't shatter glass.

Tess cheated. She cheated at cards and now she cheated me out of the position of angry, hurt and wounded sister.

I decided I'd stop speaking to her. I'd pretend we didn't go to school together with lockers down the hall from each other. I'd pretend we didn't once share a room and clothes and secrets. I'd pretend we didn't still share a history and a younger brother who spoke to insects.

Tess would be nothing more to me than a girl I sometimes saw as she was walking away or turning corners or ducking into rooms.

I took stock of my life.

I had other friends. Friends I talked to at parties or sat with at lunch. There were the people in the Environmental Club. My lab partner, Kiki Thomas. Ben from U.S. History. Natalie Banks with the stiletto-heeled boots.

Without Tess, there was nobody to talk to about Gabriel. Without Gabriel, there was nobody to talk to about Tess. Maybe that was all right after all.

And anyway, I had Dad.

Dad was always loyal—maybe not to Jane, but he was always loyal to me.

## HERE

On the first two nights Teddy goes home around ten, but on Saturday night he invents an excuse. Something about sleeping over at a friend's, and his parents buy it even though Mikey, Teddy's only real friend, is gone for the summer.

We have a whole night together.

If I complained earlier that there needs to be another word for heat down here, that the heat I've known all my life bears no resemblance to the heat I've felt since arriving in Tennessee, then the same can be said about sex.

It should have another name.

What happens with Teddy during these three nights with a room to ourselves is nothing like what happened over those months at home with Gabriel, where every time I found myself pressed against him it felt random, and every time it was over and he rolled his body away from mine, I felt the chill of insignificance envelop me.

There's nothing random about what happens with Teddy. We are here, naked together in this dingy room, exploring each other because we choose to be together, here, now.

For three days all my worries fall away. There were the worries about sex and how things would be after. And there were others too, the ones that come with sharing a small motel room with the one person in the world whom you want to see only the very best of you.

But my worries vanish into this polyester-curtained, traced-with-old-cigarette-smoke, hazy light. The days fly by in a contented blur, but at the same time, paradoxically, they go by in slow motion.

And then, when Sunday morning comes, and Teddy is lying next to me, it's like waking up from a dream. A heaviness has arrived. An intruder into this realm of new possibility. Its weight is everywhere: in the air, my hair, my T-shirt. In the comforter I kick to the floor.

Marisol returns tonight. Teddy goes back to sleeping in his trailer. In a few weeks I go back home. Everything is ending.

So maybe I'm being melodramatic. But there's something unbearably sad to me in the beautiful way Teddy sleeps with his arm up over his head and his mouth slightly open. He smells sweaty and earthy, like pencil shavings.

I trace a line from his chin down his neck, over his Adam's apple to his skinny chest, and I stop at his heart.

I stand up and walk to the window. It's late morning. The clouds are small, scattered over the deep-blue sky like someone kicked over a box of cotton balls.

"Hey," I hear Teddy say, softly and sleepily, but I don't want to turn around. I don't want him to see the tears that are starting to come against my will.

"Hey, come back here."

"It's Sunday."

"I know. Come back to bed."

"You're leaving."

He stands up and comes over and wraps his arms around me. He strokes my hair. He turns me to face him and he wipes a tear from my cheek.

"Ssshhh," he says. "Please don't cry. I can't stand it."

I laugh and wipe my face on my T-shirt. "Don't take it personally. It's me. I only manage to cry when someone treats me well."

"So if I want you to stop, I need to do my baby wrong?"

"I guess so."

We go back and sit on my bed, I lean against the head-board and he leans against the wall. I drape my legs over his lap.

He runs his hand up and down my thigh.

"I don't want you to go," I blurt out.

"I'm not sure Marisol would appreciate it if I stayed. Look at this place. I'm a total slob. I leave my clothes on the floor and toothpaste stains in the sink."

If only he'd seen the room before I'd tidied it.

"You *are* a slob. But I still wish you didn't have to go."

What I really mean to say is that I'm afraid that when he opens the door to this room and walks back to his life, some kind of spell will be broken, everything will start to fall apart, the summer will begin to end. But of course, I don't say any of that.

He kisses the top of my head. "We'll find another way to be alone," he says, completely misreading me. "There'll be other opportunities."

"Okay."

He untangles himself from me and stands up. He's all legs and arms, a stick figure in red-and-white-striped boxers. He reaches for his jeans and pulls them on. He's leaving.

He tugs his shirt over his head and leans down for a kiss, which I deliver quickly.

"I've gotta go," he says.

"Of course you do." I try to sound cool.

"You understand, right?"

"Yeah."

"No, you don't." He looks down at me and then climbs back onto the bed, pins me under him, and kisses me long and hard before he's back on his feet.

"You said it yourself. It's Sunday," he says.

"So?"

He turns back with one more smile as he reaches for the doorknob. "Jesus radio might be enough for you, but it isn't for me. I have to go to church."

He pulls open the door and light pours in.

◉ ◉ ◉

There's nobody in the breakfast room but Linus, his face obscured by a copy of the *Memphis Daily News*. I grab a banana and a muffin and I fill my travel mug with coffee.

I think about sneaking back to my room, where it still smells of Teddy, but instead I pull up a folding chair and Linus puts down his paper.

"News flash," he says. "It's going to be hot."

"I'm sick of heat. Heat totally sucks."

"Well said."

"Thank you."

"But I suggest you get used to it. It's the wave of the future, pardon the pun."

"I know it." I peel my banana but it's bruised and stringy. I put it down on the table. "Do you think we caused the tornado?" I ask him.

"You and me?"

"No, I mean humanity. Are we to blame, or do you think it was just a run-of-the-mill natural disaster?"

Linus scratches his beard. "Actually, the definition of a natural disaster is when a hazard meets human vulnerability, which pretty much accounts for all tragedies."

I think about that for a minute. *A hazard meets human vulnerability*. It does describe a lot.

What I'm really after is whether we're responsible for *this* hazard, but I know Linus doesn't have the answer. He's not a scientist, and even if he were, it wouldn't matter. Not even scientists know.

Everything is speculation.

"I haven't seen much of you this weekend," he says as he takes a final swig of his coffee before standing up and starting to clear his place. I blush. I hate breaking rules and I hate lying to Linus.

"Catching up on sleep," I offer.

I follow him to the trash bin, where I deposit my uneaten banana and the greasy paper wrapper from my muffin.

"How's Teddy?"

I look at him. Is he testing me? Does he know something?

I think of Teddy leaving, of his back as the door closed behind him and the light chased him out of the room.

I shrug. "He's fine, things are fine, I guess."

I can see Linus doesn't believe me.

What I really want to say is that nothing lasts forever, no matter how solid it seems. I know this. I've always known this. This knowledge is with me like a smooth stone in my pocket. There are days I worry my fingers over the stone's surface at every waking moment and some days I forget that the stone is there at all.

Today, the stone weighs forty pounds.

We step outside to the same cotton-ball-littered sky I saw through my window this morning while Teddy was still sleeping.

Linus closes his eyes and puts his arms out at his sides. " 'Look to this day. For it is life. The very life of life.' "

I stand beside him. Quiet.

He continues. " 'In its brief course lie all the verities and realities of your existence. The splendor of beauty, the bliss of growth, the glory of action. Today well lived makes every yesterday a dream of happiness, and every tomorrow a vision of hope.' "

He opens his eyes and looks at me. "It's an ancient Sufi text." He smiles. "My mantra."

He folds his paper, bats me over the head with it and walks away.

◎ ◎ ◎

I do another round of tidying for Marisol's return.

We're living opposite lives. Photonegatives of each other's.

Her bed is crisp and untouched, mine is a tangle. Her

clothes are folded neatly in the closet, mine are all over the floor.

She's spending a summer away from her boyfriend, but she'll go back to him soon. My boyfriend is here, just down the dusty road, but when this summer ends I'll have to say goodbye to him.

I think of Linus's mantra. In the same Eastern philosophy class where I learned about yin and yang, we read part of Ram Dass's *Be Here Now*.

Be here now.

I found the idea simplistic and annoying, which might have had something to do with the fact that Baba Ram Dass is really a Jew from Massachusetts named Richard Alpert. Or maybe it was simply that the idea that nothing else matters but the moment you're in, while an attractive idea, just didn't make any practical sense in the world I inhabited.

But Linus offers something different. More complex. An idea I can get behind. What his mantra seems to say is that if you enjoy your life in the moment, if you're happy and you live well, then that painful past begins to recede and you'll be more open to possibilities in the future.

I'm done cleaning up, and I go out into the hallway to make my weekly call to Dad.

He asks me how I am. How've I been? What's new?

What am I supposed to say? That everything has changed? That Teddy chose me? That I feel happier and more at home here than I do home alone with him?

"Nothing's new. I'm fine."

"You sound angry."

"Actually, I'm the opposite of angry."

"I'm not sure there is an opposite of angry, other than *not angry*."

I make a mental note to myself: Precision about language can be really, really annoying. It can make you miss the point of what the other person is saying altogether.

"Okay. Fine. I'm not angry, I'm happy. I'm pretty sure happiness can be an opposite of anger. And I'm happy. Things are great here."

"That's good news."

"Yes, it is. Life is good down here. My friends are fantastic. They're nice and kind and loyal. And this family we're building the house for? The Wrights? They're amazing. Teddy. And the girls. And Diane and Coach Wes. I mean, after everything they've been through, and not just the tornado, but everything, coming from different backgrounds with family who didn't approve, settling in a town that wasn't welcoming to mixed-race couples, after all that, they're still together. They've made everything work."

"That's great for them, Harper. I'm glad they're still together. I hear what you're saying. And again, I'm sorry to have failed you. I'm sorry I didn't give you the family you so desperately wanted."

"You did give it to me, Dad. And then you took it away."

There's a long silence full of clicks and scratches on the phone line.

He clears his throat and asks me about my conversation

with Jane, and whether I'm planning on calling Tess, and I tell him it's time for a meeting, which is a lie.

Baba Ram Dass was right. Linus was wrong. All I want is to *be here now*. I don't want to think about the past. I don't want to imagine what will happen when I return. I just want to protect my life here from the intrusions of that other life that is thousands of miles and clicks and scratches away.

# HOME

The story of Tess and me pretty much ends with the slamming of my car door. I wish there were more to say.

I stopped talking to her. She stopped talking to me.

There were times when this was impossible, like when I would ring the doorbell to her new house on the days Dad and I picked up Cole. Sometimes she'd say, "Hey. Hang on a sec." And then she'd walk away shouting, "Coley!"

I'd say, "Thanks."

Five words from Tess. One from me.

There was the time our U.S. History classes were joined for a one-day project. There was the time we were assigned to the same Saturday college-essay-writing workshop.

I stopped seeing Jane. I rebuffed her invitations to lunch, or the movies, or shoe shopping.

*Too much homework. I'm watching Cole. I have other plans.*

Any excuse other than *I can't face you because you remind me of too many betrayals.*

Dad tried talking to me. I never told him anything other

than I just wanted him to leave me alone, that things with Tess were hard, that he couldn't possibly understand.

But no matter what happens, the earth keeps turning.

Monday always comes and eventually, sometimes excruciatingly slowly, that Monday is followed by a Friday. You take tests and hand in papers you wrote at two in the morning the day they were due, and your shoes get worn out, and the pollen in the air increases so that you go through an entire package of tissues during the SATs, and you wander through the crowds at parties looking for Natalie Banks because you came with her, and you watch her take off for the backyard with a senior who seems to be in the backyard with a different girl at every party, and you learn to play chess with your dad, and you eat too much ice cream, and your favorite television drama has its two-hour season finale, and then suddenly the school year ends and you pack your bags for Tennessee.

And that's the end of the story.

# STEP SIX:
# THE ROOF

The summer after sixth grade I spent a month in New York City with my grandparents that flew by in a haze of melting sidewalks, Popsicles in Central Park and museum after museum. I loved sitting in the Egyptian wing of the Met. I loved cruising the design exhibit at MOMA. I loved the dizzying spiral walkway in the Guggenheim and how I could never know which floor we were on. But my favorite museum turned out to be the Frick on Fifth Avenue.

Half the reason to go to the Frick is to wander around the mansion. Now that I know a thing or two about building houses, I really appreciate the quality of the materials and the grand space. Henry Clay Frick made a fortune in steel, and after he built himself this mansion and decorated it with world-class art, he died and left it all to the public. I'm guessing that really pissed off his heirs.

My grandmother and I went once a week and we'd check out the dining room and the library, sit in the garden, and before we'd leave, I'd visit my favorite painting: *Mistress and Maid*.

One young woman in a regal yellow gown, one in a brown sack dress. One beautiful, one plain. They stand at a small writing table, pen and paper ready. There's an entire novel right there on the canvas in who these women are to each other, and how they got there.

I still remember part of the curator's description:

*There is an exceptional sense of dramatic tension in this painting of two women arrested in some moment of mysterious crisis.*

When I returned from New York, Tess had switched our beds around. Mine was now by the window. For years I'd complained about not getting enough fresh air or light in my corner of the room, but Tess wouldn't budge. Now she'd gone and surprised me, and made my bed with perfect hospital corners and moved around our bedside tables and didn't even try to pass off her lamp with the small burn mark on the shade as mine, and I knew that all of this was her way of telling me she'd missed me.

## HERE

The roof is getting shingled today. It's going to be brutal up there in this heat, and I'm hoping Linus has me inside working on the cabinets or maybe even painting.

Painting is one of the jobs nobody wants. You could go mad painting. Every wall and ceiling and inside every closet and all those corners and all that white primer and white paint, it just goes on forever, and you start to feel like you're rolling away the contents of your brain with every stroke, but it's got to be better than spending the day on the roof in hundred-degree heat.

Teddy picks me up for breakfast at his place and when we get back to his trailer, it's empty.

"Surprise," he says. He starts kissing me and we fall onto the couch. "The twins have doctor's appointments in the city." He throws some pillows to the floor. "Mom took them in for breakfast so they could beat rush-hour traffic." He pulls off my T-shirt. "Dad had an early meeting with the school principal."

"Teddy," I whisper. He stops and looks at me. "Too much information."

Later, when I'm in the bathroom, Teddy puts on the coffee and slides bread into the toaster. When I come out, smoke is filling the kitchen. He pops the toast and opens the small window over the sink and takes the butter out of the refrigerator, all as if this were the most natural thing in the world, making me breakfast after we've had sex on the couch.

*Is this love?* I wonder. *Is this what it's like? Does Teddy love me? Does pulling on his shorts and lacing up his boots before serving me burnt toast, half a grapefruit and a cup of decent coffee mean he loves me? And if so, why hasn't he told me?*

I don't know what to expect, seeing as I've never had a

boy tell me he loves me. Does he just say it? Does he pass me the boysenberry jam and say, *Would you like some jam for your toast, and by the way, I love you?*

No. He picks up the boysenberry jam, studies it and asks, "Have you ever had a fresh boysenberry? Or ever even seen a fresh boysenberry? Have you ever heard of anybody, ever, having eaten a fresh boysenberry?"

"Uh . . . no. I guess not."

"Don't you think that's weird? I mean, you can't find one jam aisle in any supermarket in this entire country without boysenberry jam in it, yet the existence of the actual boysenberry is questionable at best."

"Astute observation."

"Thanks. I think so too."

We go out to meet the bus and I bring a piece of burnt toast for Frances, because I've noticed Frances has gotten into the habit of sleeping through breakfast.

She takes a bite. "You need to work on your homemaking skills if you plan on keeping Teddy." Then she links her arm through his and they head up the path to the site.

Teddy and Frances are partners this week, and today they get the enviable job of building kitchen cabinets while I'm stuck with Seth on the dreaded roof, where it promises to be several degrees hotter than hell.

We have to seal the roof before we can shingle it, which means unfurling these huge, heavy black rolls of builders' felt from one edge of the roof to the other. The felt smells like tar.

Unfortunately, I'm wearing a white lace bra (one of the

by-products of having a boyfriend is thinking before choosing your bra), so I can't take off my shirt like Marika and Marisol. They're up here in their sports bras in what feels like some kind of cruel cosmic joke being played on Seth, who looks like he's about to pass out. It's probably just the heat. Seth isn't even looking at Marika and Marisol. There's an order to life. When you're hungry you don't worry about insignificant things, you think only of your hunger, and when you're this hot, you don't care that the two girls you've been stalking all summer are standing in front of you half naked.

Despite the heat, I keep running back over this morning's conversation with Teddy and wondering if he's ever going to tell me he loves me.

Marisol and I have taken over the eastern slope of the roof and left Seth and Marika to cover the western slope. She's unrolling the builders' felt; I'm tacking it to the roof.

"When did Pierre first tell you he loved you?" I ask.

She stops and takes the bandana off her head. She wipes her face as she thinks. I know she has the answer, but Marisol has a flair for the dramatic pause.

"The first afternoon we met. On the teen bike tour of Napa. He walked up to me and introduced himself and said that he was pretty sure he loved me, and if he hadn't been so cute I would have thought he was a psycho. But that doesn't really count, because, of course, he didn't mean it."

"So when did he tell you he loved you and mean it?" I nudge her to get back to rolling the felt, and I return to stapling it down.

"Probably the first time he tried talking me into having sex."

"How romantic."

She laughs. "Look, it didn't really matter that much because I already knew. You just know these things. Don't stress if Teddy hasn't said it yet. Just look at how he treats you. He obviously loves you."

"Really?"

"Totally."

"But why?" We've reached the edge of the roof and we stop. From up here I can see that the countryside stretches on forever. Greens and browns and yellows and little patches of life, but mostly Earth: beautiful, undestroyed, pristine Earth.

"Are you seriously asking me why you're worth loving? Are you *that* insecure?"

I don't say anything.

"Okay. Where to start?" She sits down on the roll of felt and drinks from her water bottle. "To borrow a phrase from your native land, the inferior California to the south, you are, *like, totally awesome*. Not to mention the fact that you gave up your summer vacation to come down to this sweatbox and help his family rebuild their house. And finally, because I learned in my college-essay-writing workshop that all good arguments have three prongs, I offer this: You're willing to put out."

I smile at her and cock my head.

"Your school had one of those lame workshops too?"

"No. My overbearing parents sent me to a private workshop."

"So that's how they do it in the north," I say. This time I give her more of a kick than a nudge. "C'mon, let's get back to work."

○ ○ ○

"Tell me more about Tess," Teddy says.

The cicadas are buzzing. Tonight the sky is dark and deep, and we're lying on a blanket in the grass on the hill where Teddy was planning on taking me to watch the fireworks on the night we first kissed in his truck.

I was just losing myself to the space between awake and gone, but now it's like somebody turned on stadium lights out here.

I'm alert. Sleep is a distant continent.

"What do you want to know?"

"I don't know. Anything. You know my family, but I hardly know a thing about yours."

I stop and I let myself think about Tess, really think about her, and I find I'm unable to unearth the right words.

"She hates eggs," I say.

"Really?"

"Yeah. The whole eating an embryo thing just rubs her the wrong way. Strangely, she has no problem with the full-grown chicken."

"Well, that's important to know. Thanks for that information."

He seems kind of hurt. Like I'm dodging the question. But

I'm just trying to be *here*. I'm trying to stay here, on this hillside in the dark with Teddy, and not let myself go back home.

"Teddy. I told you about what she did with Gabriel. That says everything, doesn't it?"

"Does it? Is that who she is? Someone who just does things to hurt you?"

I don't have to think about this last question for very long.

"No. She was always pretty good to me. I mean . . . she shared everything with me. Her mother, her sister, even her father. I never felt like the outsider with Tess."

I close my eyes, and I listen to the cicadas and an image comes to me: Tess in a blue-and-gold-striped soccer jersey, with mud on her knees and flushed cheeks.

"When we were nine we played in a soccer league and she was a much better player, much more coordinated and confident on the field, but when it came time for tryouts she purposely tripped over the ball and missed an easy shot on goal, and we both got put on the same midlevel team."

I watch the nine-year-old Tess run away, farther and farther down the field.

"Maybe that was just because she didn't want to get stuck playing with people she didn't know."

I open my eyes again and look at him. "That was part of it, I'm sure. But also I think she didn't want me to feel I was a crappier player than she was. Back then I was passionate about soccer, even though I wasn't very good at it."

"Sounds like she's a good sister."

"*Was.*"

"All over some guy who you were better off without anyway?"

"She knew how hurt I'd be. She had to."

He stretches his long arms back over his head. "Look, Harper, I'm obviously not a girl, so I'm a little out of my arena of expertise here, but isn't it like a cardinal rule that girlfriends, especially sisters, don't let guys get between them?"

"Yes. It is. And she broke it."

"But so did you by letting that night be the end of everything."

I'm quiet. A tickle lodges itself in the back of my throat.

"I don't think you really get it. And why should you? You have your mother and your father and your sisters. You can't be divorced out of any of those relationships."

He sits up and starts to put on his sneakers. "If you think everything is easy for me, then I don't think you know me at all," he says.

"It's not that, it's just—"

"I've been through some pretty heavy shit myself. You know?"

I sit up and grab the laces out of his hands.

"I know. I'm sorry. You're right. I know you've been through a lot. I don't mean to make it sound like your life's been easy. See? This is why I don't like talking about my family. It turns me into this wallower, wading around in my own mess, blind to everything else around me."

He's stopped, frozen with his hands stuck out in front of

him where he'd been holding his laces, and he's looking at me in a way he's never looked at me before, and for the first time since we kissed that night in his truck, I sense that he's untouchable.

Silence settles in, but not one of our comfortable silences. I hold his gaze; I don't want him to look away.

He breathes in finally, and his eyes regain their warmth and it feels like if I wanted to I could put my arms around him, but I don't.

Instead I finish tying his shoelaces for him.

"I'm sorry, Teddy. I'm really sorry."

He reaches out and strokes my hair. He takes my chin in his hand and turns my face back up to look at him.

"There's things you can fix and things you can't," he says. "And I just think it's a shame to walk away from the things you can fix."

○ ○ ○

I could write to her.

It might be easier than talking. With writing nothing gets in the way.

It feels wrong that she doesn't know anything about Teddy, or about my life down here, or about what I've learned to do and what I know now that I didn't know before.

I start to compose imaginary letters. I think about the Mistress and the Maid. I think about what they might write on that blank piece of paper between them.

If I could write to her, I might write:

Dear Tess,

Wear goggles and gloves when you use a saw. Saws are dangerous and you can never take too much care with dangerous things.

Or:

Dear Tess,

When you build a house, you build the walls flat on the ground, and when they're all done everyone gets together, because it take lots of hands, and you raise them, outside walls first, and in the space of an afternoon, what was once just a pile of lumber becomes a real home.

Or:

Dear Tess,

You can tell when a boy loves you. There's no mystery to it. And it doesn't have to do with words. I wasted too much time inventing a new version of love in which everything that didn't seem to fit could be excused or explained, but all those excuses and explanations just meant it wasn't love in the first place, it was something else.

Or:

Dear Tess,

My mother died when I was two. I've
spent my life feeling guilty that I didn't
miss her more. The only reason I didn't is
because of Jane and Rose and you, and now
that you're not who you once were, I'm
finally starting to miss her more.

PS: I'd take the guilt over the missing any
day.

◦ ◦ ◦

"We're fomenting," says Captain.

"A coup?" I ask.

"No, a plan. I looked it up, and I'm pretty sure you can
foment a plan, as long as the plan stirs up some form of
trouble."

We're sitting around in my room. I've just said goodnight
to Teddy, who went back to the trailer, and Linus did his lights-
out round of knocks, and it strikes me as a total waste that I'm
breaking the rules by letting Captain sneak into my room.

Although some rules are still being honored: Captain sits
in the armchair and Marisol stands in the doorway to the bathroom brushing her teeth. A grand total of four feet on the floor.

"The way I see it," says Captain, "our time here is coming

to an end and we've barely gotten out of this godforsaken yet charming town. We need a road trip."

"The town *is* charming," says Marisol. "And full of moxie!"

"What do you have in mind?" I ask.

"Memphis. A night out. I'm thinking a cool little club, hear some live music, drink too much, maybe puke on the sidewalk. I want to show Frances that fun can be had outside the limits of her precious city, the one with the capital C."

"I know a great place, but I think the drinking is probably out. I went there with Teddy. The music was amazing. The food was even better."

"Fine, so forget the drinking. We'll *eat* so much we puke on the sidewalk."

"Sounds irresistible," says Marisol, coming out of the bathroom in her pajamas with the eggs and bacon on them.

"So let's see if we can get permission to go Saturday night," I say.

"Where's the fun in that? Our curfew is ten o'clock. That's just when things start getting going. We'd have to leave Memphis by eight-thirty to get back here in time. And also, and I know this is a foreign concept to you, but everything is much more fun when you do it without permission." Captain takes in Marisol's pajamas. "Adorable. But you might want to consider a wardrobe change."

"*Now?*" I say. "You want to go *tonight?*"

He jumps up from the chair. "Oh, I'm sorry. Didn't I make

that clear?" He starts pacing the room. "The first thing we need is some mode of transport."

"Wait a minute. Where's Frances?" Marisol asks.

"She's putting on something hot. I told her you need to look hot when you're fomenting."

As if on cue, a quick and quiet knock arrives at the door. Captain opens it, and as he stands aside to let Frances in, he points to her with both hands.

She does a little curtsy.

"So back to the wheels . . . I was thinking we might prevail upon Teddy to borrow his dad's car."

"I don't think Coach Wes is going to go for this plan."

"Permission," snaps Captain. "This will be done without permission. Stay on the tour."

"So you mean you want Teddy to *steal* his dad's car?"

"If you want to get technical."

Marisol starts searching through her clothes.

"What are you doing?" I ask her.

"I'm changing."

Captain reaches into his pocket and pulls out a dime. He tosses it to me and I catch it.

"Go call Teddy," he says.

"When is the last time you made a call at a pay phone? 1985?" I throw it back at him. "It costs fifty cents."

"Jeez." He digs his hand into his pocket and comes up with two quarters. "No wonder everyone has a cell phone."

I sneak out into the hall and call Teddy, who goes for the

idea right away. I was counting on him refusing, which would have meant I could have gone back into the room and shrugged and said something like *Oh well, I tried*, and then I would have happily climbed into bed.

Now we're all piled into Coach Wes's car and we're flying down the dark, half-empty interstate, toward Memphis.

"Dude, thanks for doing this," says Captain from the backseat. He puts a hand on Teddy's shoulder. "You are seriously brave."

"What do you mean?" asks Teddy.

"My old man would tear me a new one if I stole his car."

"You'd probably be stupid enough to get caught. Anyway, as long as we're back before five in the morning we're good. That's when Dad gets up for his workout. Until then he sleeps like a bear in winter."

Teddy looks over at me, sniffs out my low-grade panic and smiles.

"Everything is going to be fine, Harper. Try and have a little fun."

"I'm having fun," I offer lamely, and then turn up the radio.

But as soon as we step into Alicia's, I relax. It feels good to come back here. Even though it's late on a Wednesday night, it's crowded and we have to wait a few minutes for a table. Captain strides over to the bar to order a drink, but returns carrying a Sprite.

"Told you," I say.

"Nobody likes a know-it-all," he shoots back. He reaches

into his Sprite, pulls out the maraschino cherry and glares at it.

"Like it isn't enough for the bartender to turn me down. He had to give me a cherry. It's like an extra kick in the nuts."

Teddy grabs it, pops it in his mouth and smiles. "Who knew a kick in the nuts could taste so good?"

We squeeze five chairs around a table for four right in the middle of the room just as the band is coming back to the stage from their break. Tonight there's a different trio playing drums, a guitar and keyboards, and the guys in the band look to be about a third the age of the jazz musicians Teddy and I heard last time. All three, including the white guy on keyboards, are wearing hip-hop baggy jeans, dark glasses and lots of gold, but their sound is a combination of soul, rock and jazz with just a hint of hip-hop thrown in for good measure.

They're really, really great. Did I waste my summer on Jesus radio?

Alicia comes over and smiles at Teddy and says, "So you brought some friends back, did you? Some *hungry* friends?"

"Yes, ma'am."

"Good thing," she says, and she heads for the kitchen.

"We just ate dinner a few hours ago," says Frances. "I am *so* not hungry."

"All the better for puking on the sidewalk," says Captain. He pulls her onto his lap and he kisses her neck and whispers something in her ear.

She hits him in the chest and laughs.

We get lost in the music and our conversation falls away.

I watch Teddy watching the band. His eyes are big and unblinking and he's subtly moving his body to the rhythm of the music and every now and then he shakes his head and breaks into this huge grin, like they've just let him in on an inside joke.

"These guys are outrageous," he shouts in my ear. "Amazing. I can't believe I was about to go to sleep for the night. If you hadn't called I would have missed this." He puts one arm around me and his other arm around Marisol and squeezes us.

Alicia comes back with our food, and despite the fact that, like Frances, I'm not hungry, I clean my plate. We all do.

The band breaks again just after one.

"We'll be back," says the fat guy on guitar, who also sings lead vocals. "Thanks!"

Frances looks at her watch. "They're coming on *again?* I'm impressed."

"Good luck finding a club in Providence that rocks like this on a Wednesday night," says Marisol.

"Providence?" asks Captain.

"That's where Brown is," says Frances.

"Oh, right." His face falls for just a second, but then he perks up. "Question: When Brown hears about how you spent your summer, and they admit you because they're stupid enough to think you did it out of a sense of greater good, and you move to Providence, does Providence officially become the city, or is that title still reserved for New York?"

I don't hear her answer, because an idea comes to me that's like thunder in my head.

A fabulous and slightly crazy idea. If I voiced it to the group I know how it would play out: Frances and Captain and Marisol would cheer me on and Teddy would say, *No way, uh-uh, not a chance, don't even think about it,* and then I'd have no choice but to listen to Teddy.

So instead what I do is excuse myself from the table and make like I'm going off to the bathroom.

I find the band sitting on some sofas in a small private room in the back. There's a velvet curtain I have to push aside and I stick my head in. It takes more courage than anything I've done tonight, but I take a deep breath.

The fat guy on guitar and lead vocals is called Phantom. He follows me back to the table and I introduce him to Teddy, who stands up and shakes his hand.

"You guys kick ass," says Teddy.

"Thanks, Dog," says Phantom. "So, your lady friend says you play a mean guitar."

"I'm all right," he says.

"He's awesome," says Captain. "And way too modest."

Phantom pushes his dark glasses up on his head.

"I was thinking you might want to sit in for a song or two. I'm really more of a singer, you know what I'm sayin'? I like to give it all to the vocals, so why don't you come on up and give me a break on guitar."

"No way." Teddy's look is a mix of panic and elation, but

Phantom is already pulling him by the sleeve, back toward the private room.

About fifteen minutes later they take the stage. Phantom introduces Teddy, and Teddy strikes the first few chords of a song that everyone seems to know but me. It must be a cover, because he plays effortlessly, and he's even singing some of the backup vocals.

It's late now, really late. The place is empty save for three tables and a few people sitting at the bar. I'm as excited as if Teddy were playing a sold-out show at the Staples Center.

On the way home our friends fall asleep in the backseat of Coach Wes's car.

I'm not tired.

Teddy watches the road. I watch him. He looks over at me and smiles. "What?"

I shake my head. "Nothing," I say, even though tonight was as close to the opposite of nothing as I can imagine.

We aren't home yet, the night hasn't ended, and already I'm reliving it. The sneaking out and the food and the music. Teddy on the tiny stage. The standing ovation we gave him when he returned to our table. Phantom punching Teddy's cell-phone number into his own. How Frances said this was the best night out she could ever remember having, and the extravagant bow Captain made following this pronouncement.

I think about how we can't always live in the moment because moments pass, and when we're lucky, we have the kind of moments that we can't help wanting to go back to. We think about them, remember how they felt, and when more time passes we tell stories of these moments that are worth re-living, and we tell those stories to the people we love, and tonight I find myself wishing that I could go home and tell this story, and relive this moment, and I think of Tess.

◉ ◉ ◉

Over the next few days we finish the roof. We hammer on the shingles. Siding goes up. Windows get framed in white trim with dark green shutters. The major exterior work is done, but we still have a ways to go inside. Sanding, staining, painting, hanging doors, adding fixtures and knobs and light-switch plates.

It's evening. I'm at Teddy's. Darkness is still a few hours off. I love the colors at this time of day. Gold, green, amber. The sky in Technicolor turquoise. Way off in the distance one angry cloud hangs over someplace else. Gunmetal gray.

Diane has a pot of chili on the stove with a smell so big and deep it crosses state lines. We decide to take a walk to see the house. Coach Wes stays behind to keep an eye on the chili.

"I was up there earlier." He shoots us a thumbs-up. "It's looking good."

The twins run ahead on the path, sun-streaked hair flying behind them. They've lengthened this summer. I'd forgotten how quickly your body can change on you when you're only nine years old.

They weave in and out of each other's path. Their

movements look choreographed. But it's just a natural dance of sisters who anticipate each other's next step.

They start racing around the house, peering in each window. We stand back.

"Oh, it's looking just lovely," says Diane. She places her hand on my shoulder.

Lovely might be a stretch.

The house is boxy and simple with an A-line roof. You could pass it on any street in any city or any town, and you'd probably never give it a second look. It blends in. You might call it nice, average. Not lovely.

"We wanna see our room!" shouts Alice.

"There's nothing to see yet," Teddy says.

"We don't care!"

They run inside. They've looked at the plans. They've been in the house when it was still a skeleton. They know how to find their room.

We go in after them. While Teddy takes Diane into the master bathroom to ask a question about shower tiles, I find the twins. The carpeting hasn't been installed. The floor is bare and I worry about splinters when I see them lying down on opposite sides of the room staring at the ceiling.

Without saying anything they get up and switch places.

"This way," says Alice.

"Yeah, this way," Grace agrees.

They've chosen their sides.

I sit down between them. "So what are we doing about color?"

"We want the pink we used for the fort, but Mama says no," Grace says.

Alice adds, "She thinks we'll grow out of bright pink in a minute and she doesn't want to have to repaint the room anytime soon. She says we're fickle."

"She says we have to have something neutral."

They both make a face.

I make a face too. "I hate neutral."

"Yeah, we hate neutral." Grace frowns. "What are we going to do?"

I forget about splinters and lie down like they did, flat on my back. "We'll think of something."

◍ ◍ ◍

The tornado-safe room finally gets delivered. We were expecting it a few weeks ago, and maybe it's this buildup, but somehow I imagined it as grander. It's nothing but a large metal container. A rectangular box with slits in the sides for ventilation. When I see it I find it hard to believe that everything comes down to this; that if another tornado with the same force as the one this past April hit again, this box might be the only thing left from our entire summer's worth of work.

I stand outside where the delivery truck unloaded it onto the driveway. I flip through the accompanying literature as Linus looks it over.

"Couldn't we have built a safer house?" I ask. "Why not a tornado-safe *house*? Why just a tornado-safe *room*?"

The picture on the front of the booklet shows an outline drawing of a family of five crouched together inside the container, knees pulled to their chins. A corporate idea of a typical family who looks nothing at all like the Wrights.

Just glancing at this fake family and their proximity to each other makes me claustrophobic. I toss the booklet back to Linus.

"It's kind of an exaggeration, calling this thing a room, don't you think?"

He raps the top of it with his knuckles. "This thing saves lives. We could never build a house as strong as this." He opens the door, gives it a shake. Closes it again. "At the first tornado warning you run, lock yourself in this baby, and whatever may come, you know you're gonna be okay."

"What if there's no warning?" I ask.

Linus shrugs. "Then you hang on tight and pray for the best."

It turns out that this tornado-safe "room" doubles as a kitchen island. We anchor it right in the middle of the kitchen and Linus explains that we'll cover the top with thick wooden butcher block.

I picture Diane chopping vegetables on top of this safe room. Dicing. A bowl filled with fruit. A vase with flowers. Maybe this is where the family will leave each other notes when they have something important to say.

At the end of the day I open the door and peek inside, but it's too dark in there to see a thing.

○ ○ ○

I've noticed that Captain and Frances have been bickering lately.

At lunch he called her stuck-up and she called him unsophisticated and they tried to make it seem like it was all in good fun.

Today I'm on landscaping duty. I dig my hands into the soil. I roll it between my fingers. I take my time. I'm overly careful. I try to slow everything down, to appreciate these last days, the way the earth feels in my hands.

I plant butterfly bushes, lantana and a trumpet vine that will grow someday and wrap itself around the posts of the front porch where Captain is sitting, taking a break from sanding and looking uncharacteristically forlorn.

"Everything okay with you and Frances?"

"No, not really."

"What's going on?"

"Oh nothing, other than that we're getting ready to break up."

"What? Why?"

"Because we have to. I'm going back to Florida and she's going back to that loud, noisy, disgusting city of hers and we probably won't ever see each other again."

I sit down next to him.

"Why does this have to be the end? It's you and Frances. You guys are great together. Can't you find a way to make it work?"

Captain smiles at me and gives me a playful shove. "You're sweet."

"What does that mean?"

"I mean you're naïve. This is just a summer thing. It'll always be only a summer thing. It can't be more than that. And I hate to be the one to break it to you, but it's the same for you and Teddy."

"No, it's not."

"Sure it is. Look, summer flings are great. They're easy. The saying goodbye part is a bummer, but everything leading up to that is great because you exist in this special place, this time out of time, where it doesn't matter that what happens doesn't matter."

He stops and makes a face as if he's confusing himself, but he's not confusing me. I'm having no problem following Captain. The thing is, though, I think he has it all backward.

"*Everything* matters here. What we're doing *here* matters. It's what's back at home that doesn't matter anymore."

I know how crazy I must sound, but I don't care, because what I'm saying is the absolute truth. *Look to this day, for it is life*. What matters is here and now.

"You're a great friend, Harper, so I don't mean to sit here and take a big dump on your happy parade, but did it ever occur to you to wonder why Teddy is so perfect?"

"That's just who he is."

"I'm not saying he's not a great guy, I'm just saying that you don't have to really know him, or know the difficult things about him, and you don't have to ask the questions nobody wants to ask about their own relationship, because this is all temporary. It'll be over soon enough."

I put my face in my hands. "This matters to me, Captain. It feels like the most important thing that's ever happened in my life."

He wipes his palm on his shorts and then gently rubs my back. "I'm not saying it isn't important. I'm just saying it's going to end, because it has to, and you have to go back to the real world and your real home and your real life."

*Or maybe I don't, I think. Maybe I'll just stay. Right here. In the space where new homes are built from nothing. In this place where I am finally able to be happy again.*

◎　◎　◎

On Sunday I go out into the hallway to the pay phone to make my weekly call to Dad, but instead I dial the first nine numbers of Tess's cell. I stop short of dialing the final number.

8.

There it is, right in front of me. 8. An upright infinity. With just a little more pressure from my index finger it would make a tone, the 8 would complete her number, some unfathomable network of satellites and towers would connect me to Tess. I could reach her.

Then what?

I hang up.

I read the graffiti etched into the Plexiglas of the phone shelter. I know it all by heart now. I know that KJ is a CRA-Z BTCH. I know that EVERCLEAR RULEZ!!

I dig my room key out of my pocket. I'm surprised at how easily the Plexiglas gives under its pointed tip. I carve HE+TW 4EVER.

I look at it and immediately wish I hadn't done it. I wish I'd just kept my key to myself. I've desecrated public property, and maybe even worse, I've lied to a whole generation of future pay-phone users. We won't be together forever. I'm going home soon.

I call Dad.

"It won't be long now," he says.

I sigh. "So everyone keeps saying."

"Why so down?"

"Honestly?"

"Is there any other way to talk than honestly?"

"You seem to think so."

"Ouch. I guess I walked right into that. Let's try again. What's bothering you?"

"I don't want this summer to end."

"I'm glad you're having a good time, sweetheart. You deserve it."

"No, you don't understand. I don't want to leave here. I don't want *this* to be my temporary life. My life here is better than it is back home. I want to be *here*, I want *this* to be my life."

Now Dad sighs. Long and deep. "You can't run away from your real life just because things got hard, Harper."

I let that sit there in between us for a beat.

"There's some irony in this nugget of wisdom coming from you, Dad."

"All right, that's enough now." Dad's voice is cold. Sharp. I can count on one hand the number of times he's taken this tone with me.

Dad starts to talk, another version of an apology, but one with impatient undertones. He says again how sorry he is that my life didn't turn out the way I wanted it to, that he's sorry to have let me down, but just as there are things about me I claim he can't understand, there are things about him I can't understand, and our task in this life is to love each other in spite of these things we can't understand.

I realize before Dad is done talking that I shouldn't have called him at all. He's not the one I really wanted to talk to. I'm not mad at him, I'm mad at myself for not dialing that 8. I'm mad that I'm too much of a coward to take the first step with Tess. I'm mad that I'm already missing Teddy, even though he'll be here soon to pick me up for dinner with his family.

I think ahead to the rest of my night. I'll sit through dinner and watch the Wrights, and tell myself they're perfect, when of course there's no such thing as a family who has everything, but I'll still long for something that's been gone from my life since well before October, and maybe was never there at all.

I don't know how long Dad has been done talking. How long there's been silence on the line between us.

"Dad?" I ask. "Are you there?"

"Yes, Harper. I'm here. Of course I'm here."

Monday morning I ride with Linus into Jackson to pick up the butcher block that we'll use to cover the tornado-safe room.

The highway is a flat blur of green trees. The news is on the radio, and the bits and pieces that find their way through the morning fog in my head seem to be coming from a distant land. I'm far away from everything. Nothing that this radio woman with the commanding voice and vaguely European accent says seems to have any relationship to me or to this life that I'm living.

Then she says the word *Kyoto*.

I try to tune in, but I've missed the story.

There was a time when I would never have missed a story about global climate change. But this morning I'm too lost to pay attention to the things I once cared most about.

It's ten o'clock now and the news station has turned into a country music station and I switch the dial to Jesus radio.

"Excited to go home?" Linus asks.

This feels like one of those questions that doesn't really

need an answer, like when someone asks you if you have a cold right after you've blown your nose. He's just letting me know he's caught my mood.

I answer anyway.

"Dreading it. You?"

"This is home."

He doesn't mean Tennessee, he means working on houses. I pretty much picked this up from his bio. This is what he does all the time. This is his entire life.

From the outside, it looks pretty lonely.

"What's with your tattoo?" I finally ask.

He takes his left hand off the steering wheel and he rubs the spot on his right arm where the letters are, and then he holds his hand there, squeezing it hard, until his knuckles go white.

"They're initials. *GL* and *AD*. Two people who used to mean everything to me."

I wish I hadn't asked. Despite the fact that it's written on his body, this is his private world, his history, and I've stepped into it uninvited. Are they dead? Divorced from him? Have they let a distance too big to cross grow between them?

We've exited the highway and we're pulling into the parking lot of the lumberyard.

"Some things you can never put back together again," he says, and he puts the van in park. He pulls off the big ring of keys and clips them to his belt loop.

It becomes a ritual.

I do it maybe three times a day. I dial everything but the 8.

Tonight I do it just before bed. I'm standing in the hallway in my pajamas.

I look at my graffiti in the phone booth. HE+TW 4EVER. I could easily have been writing about Tess Waxman. The lie would have been just as big.

I start to dial the numbers. I figure maybe I'll catch her working at the diner. I picture her in her uniform, balancing a tray piled high with dishes, struggling to dig her cell phone out of her apron pocket. I picture this, and it makes me smile, even though I know her phone won't ring.

When I get back to my room Teddy is there.

"Surprise," he says, and he kisses me.

I look over at Marisol.

She rolls her eyes. "He begged me to let him in, and when I said no, he offered me a dollar."

Teddy shrugs. "She's cheap. I was willing to go up to five."

I haven't seen Teddy since this afternoon. He had to help his dad sort through new gym equipment at school and get the locker room ready for preseason football.

"Nice jammies," he says. And then to Marisol, "So, how much for the room?"

"Now, *that* is going to cost you!"

Teddy laughs and I put my hand over his mouth because I hear Linus coming down the hall.

He knocks quickly.

"Goodnight!"

"Goodni-ight!" Marisol and I singsong in unison.

A few minutes pass during which Marisol and Teddy fake-haggle over how much he's going to pay her to leave us alone for a few hours, and Marisol tries to figure out whose room to crash in.

"How about Seth's?" asks Teddy.

Another knock arrives on the door. It's not the special coded knock of Captain and Frances.

We freeze. We figured Linus was long gone, so Teddy had stopped whispering, instead giving his voice over to his deep baritone.

Another knock. More urgent.

Without speaking we come to the agreement that Teddy should hide in the bathroom, and I follow him in and close the door. If Linus comes looking, I'll fake some kind of distinctly female bathroom emergency.

This plan leaves Marisol to do most of the covering up, and she's much better at this sort of thing than I am.

Teddy sits in the bathtub. I sit on the closed toilet lid. The light in the bathroom is attached to a noisy fan, so all we can hear is the door opening, some muffled voices. Not Linus. It's probably Susannah. That's a relief. I'd much rather be caught by Susannah.

The door to our room closes again.

There's a pause and then Marisol knocks on the bathroom door. "Harper, I think you might want to come out here."

She sounds serious.

I open the door, and there, in my motel room, like an

apparition, staring at me with eyes the color of Tennessee grass, is Tess.

I step out of the bathroom, Teddy behind me.

We stand there, like four opposing points on a compass, all staring into the middle.

I recall the image of Tess that came to me only minutes ago: in a fifties waitress uniform, juggling trays of french fries and milk shakes. I put that image of awkward Tess up next to the Tess who stands calmly before me, her loose hair falling over her shoulders. Her pale blue button-down shirt and jeans. Her flip-flops. Her perfectly pedicured toenails.

I know I should say something, but I don't know what to say.

"I'm Teddy." He breaks the silence. He sticks out his hand. Tess shakes it. "And I don't usually hang out in the bathroom."

"Tess," she says in a voice that betrays her. She's not calm and confident. She's nervous.

"Nice to meet you, Tess. I was just leaving."

"Me too," says Marisol. "I'll be in Frances's room, probably dashing Captain's hopes for make-up sex."

Teddy gives my shoulder a squeeze and we exchange a look that is so familiar, so filled with understanding, that even with everything happening in this moment, I think: *Remember his face, remember how he knows you, you'll want to be able to remember this someday.*

I sit down on the edge of the bed as Teddy leads Marisol out the door. It closes quietly behind them.

"Nice place," Tess says.

I smile, but then suddenly I'm irritated that I let her get off this cheap joke. Who is she to make fun of this room? This is where I live.

"No, I mean it," she says. "It's cozy."

She takes a seat in the armchair.

I look at her. She's walked in here without anything. She doesn't have a purse or a jacket or her cobalt blue suitcase that matches mine, gifts to us from Jane two Hanukkahs ago. She's walked in here like she lives just down the hall, which I then learn, she actually does.

"I flew to Chicago to meet Rose. Her friend took a plane back home. Rose agreed to drive me down here to see you. We checked in about half an hour ago." She pauses. "Our room smells."

*Rose is here!* I think, but I still don't say anything. I fold my legs underneath me on the bed.

"You look good," she says, and fixes her eyes on me. She picks up a pen from the table next to her and passes it absent-mindedly from one hand to the other. "Tan. Your hair has gotten even lighter. You look healthy. And I'm not just saying all this so you'll talk to me instead of just sitting there staring at me like that."

"You look good too," I say. But this isn't a news flash.

"And I'm guessing that the bathroom boy, Teddy, is your boyfriend?"

I nod.

"He seems really nice."

"He is. I like him. A lot. So do you think maybe, just as a small favor to me, you could refrain from sticking your tongue in his mouth?"

"I can try," she says, a slow smile spreading on her face.

"Good."

She turns serious. "About that . . ."

"Forget it."

"I can't. And clearly you can't either. I should have told you I'm sorry."

"You *should* have told me?"

"God. Do you always have to be the grammar police? What I mean to say is I should have told you *earlier,* and I'm telling you now. I'm sorry. I shouldn't have done that. I knew how you felt about Gabriel, and I don't really have a great explanation other than that I was stupid. And angry. Really upset about everything, about Art and what happened with Mom, and you're so much like him, not that you're dishonest, I mean you *look* so much like him, and you just make me think about him and what he did to Mom and all of us, and I wanted to hurt him, but I hurt you instead, and is this making any sense at all?"

"Sort of," I say. I think about launching into a defense of Dad, a speech about how it's too easy to blame him for everything, but I also understand that what is happening right now between us is delicate and this probably isn't the best moment for speeches.

"And Gabriel never treated you right. He was a decent

friend a long time ago, but all that fooling around or what-ever, and he'd be with other people, and, I don't know, I think he could have been more clear," she says. "I probably did you a favor."

"Easy there. Don't go making yourself into a martyr."

"You're right. Sorry. I just needed to say that, because I've always thought it and never said it. I never liked the way he treated you. You loved him. He must have known that. And you were good to him, you would have been good for him, be-cause that's who you are, and he took advantage of you."

I get up and go over to my closet. I don't feel right sitting here in my pajamas, but I don't feel like changing in front of her either. So I grab some clothes and put them in a pile next to me on the bed, and I just let them sit there.

"What are you doing here?" I ask. "How did you even know how to find me?"

"Mom told me. She really misses you. She still makes zuc-chini bread sometimes, even though you were the only person in the family who ever liked it. The loaves sit on the counter until they're hard as bricks."

Something hurts right behind my rib cage. I try to breathe into the pain, but that only makes it spread. A dull ache. It's the space in there that hurts. The space where everything used to be.

"Anyway, Mom told me to come see you. She says the best way, the only way, to work out your problems is to talk them through face to face. To not let too much time go by, where they grow so big it's too late for talking. Rose agreed to drive me. And I came, even though I didn't think you'd want me here."

"I slept with Gabriel."

She stares at me and gnaws away at her lower lip. "I didn't know."

"I know you didn't."

"I wouldn't have . . . Oh my God. That would have changed—"

I cut her off. "It doesn't matter anymore."

She sits on Marisol's bed, facing me. I think about the nights when we'd talk from our beds on opposite sides of the room, whispering in the dark, when the only space between us was a few feet of striped carpet.

"I thought he was what I needed," I finally say. "I just needed somebody."

I pick up the pile of clothes next to me and take them into the bathroom. I close the door.

"Can you get the keys to Rose's car?" I call over the sound of the fan.

"Sure. Why?"

"Because," I say, "I have something I want to show you."

We park the car near the trailers and I can see by the light inside that the Wrights are still awake. I'm pulled toward them; I want to walk up the steps, open the door and blend right into their night, become a part of all they do just before going to bed.

Instead I walk with Tess up the path to the building site, guided by a weak flashlight's beam. Tess stumbles over a rock. I instinctively throw out my arm and she catches it to stop herself from falling. It's the first time we've touched in so long.

When we reach the house I try to illuminate it for her, but the flashlight just isn't up to the task.

Then I remember that the electricity works. This isn't a building site anymore; it's a real house.

"Stay here," I say, and take the porch steps two at a time. The front door is unlocked, there isn't anything inside yet to steal. Anyway, Bailey isn't a place where people lock their doors.

I flip on the outside lights.

Tess smiles and applauds and she looks like she did at her seventh birthday party when Professor Funster took a needle the length of a ruler and put it through a purple balloon without popping it.

"It's amazing. It really is. You did this?"

I'm standing next to her now, looking up at the white house with dark green shutters and a black-shingled roof.

This house doesn't look *nice, dependable, average*. Tonight this house is lovely.

"Well, I had some help."

"You really did this. You decided it was what you wanted to do with your summer and you went and did it. You know what I did? I studied SAT practice tests and served overpriced burgers to B-list celebrities."

"I heard. I want to see the uniform sometime."

"It's a sight to behold."

I stop for a moment to soak up the sound of the cicadas. I'm so used to them now that I almost don't hear them anymore, and I don't want to miss out on one of my last chances to listen to their night music.

"I wish I could have done better," I say.

"With what?"

I nod at the house. "The house. It's for Teddy. I wish I could have built him the Frick."

Tess has heard me go on about the Frick. I sent her a postcard that summer of *Mistress and Maid*.

"Can I see the inside?" she asks.

"Sure. It's not finished yet, but we're almost there." I lead her up the front steps and when we get to the door I stop. "Take off your shoes." I start to take off mine.

"Did you just do the floors or something?"

"No," I say. "This is a home. We are walking on sacred ground."

# STEP SEVEN:
# FINAL TOUCHES

◆ver the next two days we finish.

Everything is done, and every trace of us having even been here is gone. The work sheds and the portable toilets and the trucks and the extra materials and the trash. Everything has disappeared. Even the driveway up to the site, those well-worn dirt tire tracks, has been paved over with fresh asphalt. The only sign left that I spent my summer building a house is the house itself.

Tess chipped in. She helped clear debris and clean the paint splatters off the hardwood floors and patch holes in the walls left by the electricians. Rose spent the days by the pool reading magazines and talking on her cell phone, but Tess wanted to help.

I canceled my flight home to catch a ride with them. I'd

have days in the car between here and there. It would ease the transition.

I had to lend Tess some clothes. She brought only tight jeans and a few summer dresses, so she wore my shorts and T-shirts and she complained that she looked like a she-male, but of course she looked fabulous, her hair tied up over her head and her cheeks naturally rosy.

At lunch we'd sit around eating our soggy sandwiches with an absence of taste I no longer minded, and Tess would talk with my friends, who had stockpiled an arsenal of questions for her. They were mostly about when I first started showing signs of the Girl Scout I was to become.

"No," Tess tells them. "Harper never *actually* joined the Girl Scouts, but I always figured that was because she was afraid the cookies would rot her teeth."

"Ha. Ha. Ha," I say.

On the second-to-last night here, Tess convinces me to do something I haven't done all summer. I show up for a midnight swim at the pool.

Teddy comes too. The night is clear and the stars are bright. Captain and Frances have put their end-of-the-summer bickering behind them and he holds her in his arms in the pool, where you could get tricked into thinking he's unusually strong, but then you remember that it takes no effort at all to hold someone up when you're both standing in water.

As usual there are boys circling Tess. There's Jared, who broke up with Stacey two weeks ago, and Seth, who doesn't seem to have let an entire summer of rejection discourage him in any way.

Tess ignores them. We have a lot of catching up to do.

We sit side by side on lounge chairs. I watch as Teddy does a running cannonball jump, and his body sails through the air like he was made to fly, and he lands with a ferocious splash and then is scolded by a chorus of harsh whispers. Cannonballs aren't cool when you're sneaking into the pool at midnight. I can see from the way he smiles that he knew he was causing trouble when he took the leap.

"He's great," Tess says. "Really great. They don't grow them like that where we're from."

"I know," I sigh.

"How are you doing with the whole getting-ready-to-say-goodbye thing?"

"I'd say I'm failing miserably." I lean my chair all the way back so I'm looking up at the night sky. "I don't want to go home."

"I can't imagine you would."

I love that the first thing out of her mouth isn't that I'm crazy or that even if I don't want to, I have to go home again.

"I just don't know how to deal."

"It'll be okay," she says.

"And then there's Teddy . . ."

"I know."

I think I see a shooting star, but I can't be sure. It happened so fast.

"Do you remember my bat mitzvah?" she asks.

"Are you kidding?"

"I'm totally not. Did you pay any attention to my speech?"

"I was concentrating on not dying of boredom. I guess I tuned everything else out."

"I worked hard on that, and if you weren't even listening, who was?"

I just look at her.

"Right. Nobody."

"I'll listen now. Give it another go."

"Like I could even remember it. I was thirteen. But I do remember I talked about this thing that this famous rabbi wrote once about how Christians build cathedrals, these gorgeous impressive structures, but Jews, with a long history of watching their buildings get destroyed, build their cathedrals in time. The High Holidays. Shabbat. Cathedrals carved out of time that can never be torn down. I know you're no Jew, but I kind of think that's what you did with your summer down here."

I feel like I could give myself over right now to a big cry. I could lose myself in the sorrow of the goodbyes that haven't been said yet, or the changed life I never invited that awaits me back at home. Instead I look around me at everyone having a great time.

"You think we could take them?" I motion toward the pool, where Frances is sitting on Captain's shoulders and Marisol has climbed onto Teddy's and they're having a chicken fight.

We're up and stripping down to our bathing suits.

"I haven't been in a chicken fight since elementary school."

"You can sit on me," I offer.

"I wouldn't have it any other way."

We jump in and get eliminated almost immediately and we come up for air and we laugh.

By the time I walk Teddy to his truck it's already four-thirty in the morning. The sun will be up in less than two hours. He leans with his back against the door and I lean on him. He starts to pull away, but I hold him tighter and then I release him. He climbs in and unrolls his window and kisses me once more from the driver's seat.

I gesture to the hood.

"You really should have this thing fixed."

"Someday," he says. He turns on the ignition and pulls away slowly. I stand outside staring up the road until I no longer can see his taillights.

I stand there for a few more minutes. Finally I go back to my room, and since it's too late to bother with sleep, I begin to pack.

○ ○ ○

Today, our final day, is move-in day. Tonight there will be a party, but first we have some heavy lifting to do.

Most of the Wrights' belongings, the things that survived the tornado, have been sitting in a storage unit in Jackson. As we move their furniture, their lamps and their boxes off the truck—careful to lift with our knees, not our backs—I see for the first time all the things that make their home their home.

There's a corduroy armchair that reminds me of one we used to have in our house, which Jane took with her when she moved out and had re-covered in brown Ultrasuede. I used to sit in it and read and rest my feet on Pavlov.

We move new beds into the twins' room. Grace's on the left, Alice's on the right. The walls are a color called Eggshell, but Teddy and I used the leftover bright pink paint from the fort in the woods to paint the inside of their closet. And also, we painted a thick pink line up one wall, across the ceiling and down the other Eggshell wall.

"Ooohhh! Look at our closet! And I love the stripe!" Grace jumps up and down.

"What's it for?" Alice asks.

I shove her bed into place. It fits just inside the bright pink line.

"That's where the invisible wall goes."

I help Teddy set up his room. I fold his clothes and arrange his guitars on the built-in stands. I step back as he holds the Miles Davis poster up over his bed, and I try my best to tell him if one side is higher than the other.

When we're done I don't know where to sit. Teddy stretches himself out on his bed. He kicks off his shoes. He motions for me to come over and lie down next to him.

I shake my head. It doesn't feel right. This is Teddy's room and I don't belong here.

"Just for a minute," he says. "Please."

I shake my head again. My throat starts to constrict. I open the door to leave and he follows me in his socks.

The house has cleared out now. It's lunchtime. Everyone is outside and I'm going out to join them. Outside. Where I belong.

I head for the front door, but then Teddy grabs me by a belt loop on my shorts and pulls me into the kitchen.

"What's wrong?"

I don't want him to see me cry, so I put my hands over my face.

"In here," he says. He crouches down, opens the door to the tornado-safe room and climbs in. I look in after him, but all I can see are the whites of his socks. The claustrophobic in me is screaming to run away.

But I climb in and shut the door and it's blacker than night in here and Teddy finds me, wraps his arms around me and kisses my eyelids and then my lips.

"I'm going to miss you," he says. "You know that, don't you?"

I think about the literature that came with this room. Those outlines of people huddled together. The pamphlet didn't lie. Just being in here makes me feel safer.

"Thanks for everything," I say.

"*You're* thanking *me?*"

"Yes. If I forget to say that later, if I get moody or sad or I have such a hard time saying goodbye that I don't say anything at all, I wanted to make sure that I thanked you for everything. Thanks for choosing me, for wanting to be with me, and thanks for making the rest of my life fade away at a time when I needed to stop thinking about the rest of my life, and thanks for reminding me that I couldn't keep going on like that, not thinking, and thanks for helping me start talking to Tess again. Thanks for loving Jesus radio as much as I do. And thanks for the pie."

"Harper, I . . ."

"You don't have to say it."

"I don't?"

"I know."

"You know what?"

I lean against him, nestling in the crook of his arm. I talk into his neck. I don't need to be able to see to find the parts of him I know.

"That morning in the trailer, when we had it to ourselves, and you made me breakfast, I wondered whether you would tell me you loved me, if you'd ever tell me, and I looked at you, and I thought you were going to say it, but instead you went off on a tangent about boysenberry jam."

"And?"

"And it was funny. And it was close enough to the real thing for me. Just sitting there with you like that."

"Boysenberry jam?"

"Boysenberry jam."

"Harper," he whispers into my hair.

"Yeah?"

"I boysenberry jam you."

The party is on the lawn out behind Teddy's house. This is the same spot where we had our first lunch with the Wrights, when Diane brought us a picnic and it felt like we were eating in the middle of nowhere. But it's a backyard now, neatly landscaped with a smattering of pink hibiscus, and small white lights that twinkle at night like distant planets.

If things were different, this would be a night where we all dressed up. The girls in strapless chiffon gowns, the boys in tuxedos. This is our big night. But we have nothing with us other than our T-shirts and shorts and work boots and jeans, and the best we can do is to wear something clean.

Teddy's friend Mikey, his one true friend, returned from his summer away in time for the party. When Teddy introduced us, Mikey smiled and shook my hand and said how nice it was to meet me. But he also looked at me like: *Who are you?*

I wasn't sure how to respond to that.

We write messages in each other's notebooks. Inside jokes we probably won't remember by next summer. We make certain we have each other's e-mails, cell phone numbers.

Marisol is coming down from San Francisco in October, so we pretend that we don't even need to say goodbye, and we end up ignoring each other all night, but I watch as she takes Seth aside and says something to him, and he smiles, and she then delivers a quick kiss right to his lips.

I well up when Captain hugs me. I've never been to Florida and I can't imagine when I'll ever go. He hugs Tess too, even though they've only known each other a few short days, and over her shoulder he shoots me a perverted look as he makes a fake grab for her ass.

We dance under the stars. I dance with Coach Wes. I hold hands with Alice and Grace as they jump up and down with no relation at all to the song's tempo. I find Linus by the punch bowl and I ask for his e-mail to add to my book, but he gives me a look to remind me that he is a man of no address.

"You know," he tells me, "next summer there's a project planned in Ecuador. Up in the mountains near Quito. As long as you don't have trouble with altitude sickness, I'd love to have you in on that. And I was thinking maybe Teddy could do it too. You'll be college age by then. You could be chaperones. Both of you. Do you think you could handle making sure everyone's where they're supposed to be when the lights go out?" He smiles at me. We stand facing each other and then he makes a move as if to hug me, but instead reaches out and musses up my hair.

Teddy comes over and pulls me onto the dance floor. It's a slow song. He wraps both his arms around me and we hardly move.

The only thing around us, above us, is sky. Cathedrals in time have no walls. They have no roof.

"Guess who called me today?" he asks.

"The admissions director at UCLA. He called to say they're holding a spot for you, but the dorms are full, so you'll have to live at my house."

"Nice guess." He pats my back. "No college this year.

Next year for sure. But this year is about the clinic. And . . ." He pulls back and looks at me with a big expectant smile.

"And . . . what?"

"Phantom called. They have a gig next week at a club in Nashville and he wants me to play. I start rehearsal the day after tomorrow."

The music has changed from slow and quiet to loud and frenetic, but I hardly hear it. Right at this moment there is nothing here, nobody but Teddy.

"Who's the man?" he asks.

"You are." I tighten my arms around him.

We've already said our goodbyes, even though we still have tonight. We still have the morning. There's breakfast. There's the time it'll take to pack up the car. I've said goodbye to Teddy and it feels good to have that out of the way so that now I can just look at his face and take pleasure in how much he's looking forward to next week. The good things that will still be here after I'm gone.

We've made promises. We'll talk. We'll write. He'll come visit me after the clinic is built. The truck can make the trip, he swears. He likes long drives. He's always wanted to see the Painted Desert. It's a bit out of the way, but so what? I can come visit, anytime I want. His family loves me, he says.

I tell him Cole would like him, and Dad too. There's a Mexican restaurant that will blow him away. The ocean is warm enough for swimming only in the summer; it's a common misconception that Californians go to the beach all year round. I've heard about this club on Fairfax that has great music, and I'll be eighteen soon enough, so I'll be able to take him there. Pavlov likes to hike in the mountains and sometimes we see rattlesnakes. Teddy should make sure to bring his boots.

I'd like to believe all this. That our plans will happen. That we'll meet again, in the Painted Desert or high in the mountains of Ecuador. I'd like to believe that we're just beginning to build something, and that we'll make it happen. I *do* believe it. At least, I do tonight.

# HOME

We're crossing over the Mississippi River.

We've left Tennessee for Arkansas.

I'm looking at the map, big and unruly across my legs. Tess is driving. Rose is stretched out in the backseat. We have only four more states to travel through before we reach California.

"What is this crap?" asks Tess.

She's referring, of course, to Jesus radio.

"Trust me," I say. "Just give it a chance."

I think about my trip here, how I looked out the window and watched the earth changing color. I'll get to see it now in reverse. It's still summer; the landscape won't be much different. Those greens and browns and reds are waiting. Even in this era of climatic crisis, change takes place slowly, not over the course of twelve weeks.

I'm looking forward to the trip. To taking our time. To seeing the things you can't see from thirty-five thousand feet.

I turn up the radio.

It's still early enough in the day to have our windows down. I try to fold up the map, but the wind keeps whipping it around. You have to be some kind of structural engineer to figure out how to return it to its rectangular shape, so I bunch it up and throw it into the backseat at Rose, who grumbles about trying to sleep.

We don't really need the map. Home is pretty much a straight shot from here.

One way or another, we'll find the road back.

## About the Author

Dana Reinhardt lives in San Francisco with her husband and their two daughters. She is the author of two previous novels, *A Brief Chapter in My Impossible Life* and *Harmless*.